stories

Goopy Gyne Bagha Byne and Other Stories

UPENDRAKISHORE ROYCHOUDHURY

Translated from the Bengali by SWAGATA DEB

Illustrated by Dipankar Bhattacharya

INTRODUCTION BY RUCHIR JOSHI

PUFFIN BOOKS
An imprint of Penguin Random House

PUFFIN BOOKS

USA | Canada | UK | Ireland | Australia
New Zealand | India | South Africa | China

Puffin Books is part of the Penguin Random House group of companies whose addresses can be found at global.penguinrandomhouse.com

Published by Penguin Random House India Pvt. Ltd
4th Floor, Capital Tower 1, MG Road,
Gurugram 122 002, Haryana, India

Penguin Random House India

First published in Puffin by Penguin Books India 2004
This edition published 2015

10 9 8 7 6 5 4 3

ISBN 9780143333814

Typeset in Minion Pro by Manipal Digital Systems, Manipal

Printed at Repro India Limited

www.penguin.co.in

FSC www.fsc.org MIX Paper from responsible sources FSC® C047271

CONTENTS

TALES OF BIRDS

TALES OF FOXES

TALES OF A CAT

INTRODUCTION

It's hard to remember that our parents were once children. And it's almost impossible to imagine our grandparents as kids, playing in the mud, shouting loudly as children do, getting their faces dirty and scraping their knees. The stories in this book are written by a man who never quite lost from within the mischievous kid he once was, who kept that kid jumping and playing pranks even when he was a much older person.

Upendrakishore Roychoudhury was a man who was deeply interested in the world. He was a man who could do many different things: he learned to print books and then developed his own technology to improve the printing learn and develop technology for printing books, draw and paint and so on. He was a man of many talents but he's now best remembered as a master of the short tale, the magical yarn that draws you in, makes you laugh, makes you wonder, makes you scared and worried for the characters and then makes you happy.

Upendrakishore Roychoudhury might seem like a long name to some people; today he might have been called something like Upen Roy-C, but let's call him by his initials, URC. So what this URC shares with many of the great storytellers who wrote stories meant for kids is a love of life, a vivid imagination, and a great command of simple but beautiful language. Like the Grimm Brothers, Lewis Carroll and, more recently, Roald Dahl, URC wrote stories that have entered the very dna of the language in which they were written—in his case Bangla—so that people refer to his characters by way of a shorthand, like you would use a well-known smiley icon in text message. URC also started the first Bangla children's magazine, *Sandesh*, that his son, his grandson and now great-grandson have continued to publish.

URC picked up many Bengali folktales, stories usually told orally and passed down generations, polishing them into little gems of printed text, such as the *Tuntuni* stories. At the same time URC also wrote many original stories, the most well known of which is *Goopy Gyne Bagha Byne* which gives the title to this book. I won't tell you too much about this great, funny, touching magical yarn (and if you happen to be Bengali, and of a certain age, you won't need me to tell you anything) except to say that URC was the first of a very remarkable three generations of artists. His son Sukumar Ray (he dropped the Choudhury part of the surname) also wove his way into a great and happy place in Bengali culture, producing the superbly funny pieces of children's writing *Abol Tabol*, *HaJaBaRala* and *Pagla Dashu*. Sukumar died at quite a young age, thirty-six, when his son Satyajit was only two years old. This Satyajit grew up to become what many consider to be India's greatest film-maker.

The reason *Goopy Gyne Bagha Byne* is known outside Bengal is because Satyajit made one of his most brilliant films, a full-length feature film, out of this great short story. Now that the story is available in this lovely translation by Swagata Deb, and with its superb illustrations, I would urge you, if you haven't seen the film, to wait and read the story before you see it. Think, if you will, of the story and the film as two very different but related magical creatures. This book is marker of the beginning of a great line which begins with Upendrakishore and gives us the gift of the hugely multi-talented Satyajit.

Ruchir Joshi
Dec 2015

TALES OF MEN

GOOPY GYNE BAGHA BYNE

This is the story of a man who could sing only one song.

His name was Goopy Kyne, son of Kanu Kyne the grocer. Goopy could sing only *one* song, but no one else in the village could sing anything at all. That is why they called him Goopy Gyne ('gyne' means 'singer').

Although Goopy could sing only one song, he sang it all the time! He couldn't spend a single minute without singing. If he wasn't singing, he felt as if he couldn't breathe. When he sat in his father's shop and sang, all the customers would run away. When he sang in the fields, all the cows would tear their ropes and flee. Soon people stopped coming to his father's shop. All the cowherds stopped taking their cows to the fields.

One day Kanu Kyne decided he had had enough. He chased Goopy out of the house with a thick rod. Goopy ran to the fields. There the cowherds came running at him with sticks. Finally, he escaped into the forest and started practising his song very hard.

In another village close by, there lived a man called Panchu Pyne. Panchu's son loved playing the drum. While playing his drum, he would shake his head, tap his feet, glare at everyone, gnash his teeth and frown fiercely. People in his village would gape at him and marvel 'Aaa-aah! Oo-ooh!' Sometimes he would let out a RRRROAR, just like a tiger. When he did that, his audience would run away in fear and stumble and fall! That is why he was known as Bagha Byne (which means 'the tiger-like drummer'). Everyone forgot what his actual name was.

Bagha would start playing his drum with gusto every morning, and so great was the force of his playing that he would also break the drum by the end of each day. His father would have to buy him a new one the following morning.

In the end, Panchu Pyne could not afford to buy Bagha any more drums. But how could Bagha give up drumming? People in his village said, 'We will all collect money to supply Bagha with drums. It is our good fortune to have such an accomplished drummer in our village. He shouldn't stop playing.'

After much discussion, they decided that they would buy him a drum that was so strong and sturdy that even Bagha would find it difficult to break.

And what a drum they bought for him! It was three-and-a-half feet wide, equally tall, and its skin was made from buffalo-hide! Bagha was overjoyed. 'I'll play it standing up,' he said.

So from that day Bagha played his drum standing up. The drum had a fine sound. It was not only marvellously loud, it was also amazingly strong and remained undamaged even after Bagha played it day and night for one-and-a-half months.

But his parents' heads started throbbing from listening to him, and they thought they would lose their minds. All the other people in the village also started feeling dizzy in the head. No one can say what could have happened if this went on much longer.

One day all the villagers came armed with big sticks and told Bagha, 'Dear brother, we will give you ten pots of sweets. Please go somewhere else. If you stay here, we'll all go mad!'

Poor Bagha! What could he do? He had to take his drum and go to another village. They heard him play and greeted him enthusiastically.

But within two days, the people of that village also threw him out. After that, wherever he went, he was driven out in no time.

Bagha started roaming the fields. When he felt hungry, he would go back to his village and start drumming. The villagers would quickly bring him food and heave a sigh of relief when he left! But soon they stopped bringing food. They brought sticks instead.

'Enough is enough,' thought poor Bagha. 'It's better to go and live in the forest than to suffer fools. What can happen? I may get eaten by a tiger. But at least I'll be able to play my drum.' And he went into the forest with his drum.

Bagha lived quite happily there for some time. He could play his drum without people chasing him with sticks. But after a while, his peace was disturbed. The forest had no tigers, but it did seem to have one Terrible Beast! Bagha hadn't seen it, but he had heard it roar in the distance. Its bellow would make him tremble all over. 'This creature will probably eat me up and my drum too if he sees me!' Bagha thought, and decided he should find another forest to live in.

The terrible beast was none other than Goopy Gyne! What Bagha thought was the beast's roar was Goopy practising his song in another part of the forest!

Goopy could also hear Bagha playing the drum and he too was terrified by its loud roar. Finally, one day, he decided to run away from the forest. He could not live in fear of the beast.

As he was making his way out, he saw another man carrying an enormous drum on his head. Goopy was amazed to see him. 'Who are you?' he asked.

'I am Bagha Byne. Who are you?' said Bagha.

'I am Goopy Gyne. Where are you going?' asked Goopy.

'I'll go wherever I can find a place to stay,' Bagha replied. 'All the people in my village are idiots. They can't appreciate good music. That is why I came to stay in the forest. But there is a terrible beast here. If I stay here, the creature will surely eat me, and my drum too. That is why I am going away.'

'You are right,' said Goopy. 'I was also running away from this beast. Tell me, where did you hear it roar?'

'From the east,' said Bagha. 'From the bamboo thicket.'

'Why, that was me!' cried Goopy. 'You heard my song! That wasn't the beast! The beast roars on the western side of the forest, by the big banyan tree.'

'That was the sound of my drum!' said Bagha. 'I was playing it under the banyan tree.'

As they realized that they had got scared listening to each other's music, they burst out laughing.

Then Goopy said, 'I am a Gyne and you are a Byne. I am sure that the two of us can do great things together.'

Bagha agreed. They decided that they would go and play for the king. Who knows, pleased with their music, the king might even give them each half his kingdom and a daughter as bride!

Goopy and Bagha felt very happy now that their future was sorted. They laughed and sang and danced on their way to the king's palace. After some time, they reached the bank of a wide river. The palace was on the other side.

There was a boat to take people across the river, but the boatman wanted money. Goopy and Bagha had spent the last few days in the forest. Where could they get money?

'We can't pay you,' they said to the boatman. 'But we can sing and play music for you. We are great musicians, we are going to play for the king. Please take us across the river.'

The other passengers liked the idea. 'We'll pay for them. Let them come along,' they told the boatman.

The boatman was also eager to hear their music. He agreed at once. Goopy and Bagha got on the boat, and the boatman started rowing.

The boat was packed with people. There was no space for Bagha to put down the drum. But once the passengers realized this, they huddled closer and made space for Goopy and Bagha in the centre of the boat.

By this time, the boat had reached the middle of the river. After humming a little to clear his voice, Goopy started to sing his one song and Bagha started playing the drum.

Everyone was so alarmed by the sound that they all jumped up from their seats and the boat turned over, depositing all the passengers in the river.

Goopy and Bagha were now in deep trouble. Luckily, Bagha's drum was so big that they could hold on to it tightly and stay afloat. But they could not guide the drum so it floated down the river with the tide. They didn't reach the king's palace, but as the day ended, the drum came to a stop by a thick jungle.

The jungle would have been frightening enough in the day. At night, it was simply TERRIFYING!

'Things look bad, Goopy,' said Bagha. 'What should we do now?'

'Why, I will sing and you will play the drum,' said Goopy. 'Since we are surely going to be eaten up by a tiger, we might as well show it how talented we are.'

'You are right!' agreed Bagha. 'If we have to die, we should die like heroes and not like some village bumpkins!'

The two of them started their concert. Bagha's drum was wet. It produced a deep and rumbling sound. Goopy's voice was also sombre and mournful because he thought it was going to be his last song. So the music turned out to be quite grand. They performed for an hour or two. It was past midnight, but the two of them could not stop playing.

Though they were both completely wrapped up in the music, suddenly they sensed that there was something happening around them. Big, black, shadowy shapes seemed to be peering at them from the tops of the trees. These shapes had eyes that glowed like lamps and teeth that gleamed in the dark.

Goopy and Bagha huddled close together in fear and wonder, forgetting their music. Their backs were hunched, their eyes popped out, and their mouths hung wide open. They were trembling so hard and their teeth were chattering so loudly that they could not even run away.

The shadowy shapes were ghosts!

But these ghosts did not want to harm them in any way. They had in fact been listening spellbound. They liked the

music so much that they wanted to ask Goopy and Bagha to play at their king's son's wedding. So when the music stopped, they complained in banshee-like tones, 'Why did you stop, dearies? Go on playing, go on!'

Goopy and Bagha felt a little better when they heard the ghosts speak. 'This doesn't sound too bad,' they thought. 'Let's carry on and see what happens.'

As soon as they started their song again, one by one the ghosts climbed down from the trees and started dancing around them!

What a performance it was! Goopy and Bagha had never had such an appreciative audience. The musicians and the ghosts sang and danced the whole night through.

All too soon, the eastern sky started to lighten. Ghosts can't stay out during the day. Just before daybreak, they said to Goopy and Bagha, 'Come home with us. We will take good care of you.'

'We have to go to the king's palace,' said Goopy.

'You can go there later,' said the ghosts. 'Come to our home and play some music there first.'

Goopy and Bagha couldn't refuse. They went along with the ghosts and played some more music. When bidding them farewell, the ghosts said, 'Tell us what you want.'

'All we want is to please people with our music,' said Goopy.

'So be it,' said the ghosts. 'Once you start singing, no one will be able to move before your song is over. What else do you want?'

Goopy thought for a while and said, 'We should always have enough to eat and decent clothes to wear.'

The ghosts handed them a bag and said, 'Whenever you want something to eat or a new set of clothes, just put your hand into the bag. You will get it. What more do you wish for?'

Goopy scratched his head and said, 'I can't think of anything else.' Bagha could not either.

The ghosts smiled and gave them two pairs of shoes. 'Whenever you want to go anywhere, just put on these shoes and say where you want to go. They will take you there.'

Goopy and Bagha now had nothing to worry about. All that they could ever need had been provided for.

They thanked the ghosts, and bade them farewell. Then they put on their magic shoes and said clearly, 'We want to reach the king's palace.'

The jungle around them disappeared, and they found themselves before the gates of a huge mansion. They had never seen such a magnificent house. They knew at once that they had reached the palace.

But there was a problem.

The gates were guarded by two fierce men who looked like demons from hell. When they saw Goopy and Bagha with his drum, they gnashed their teeth and said, 'Halt! Where do you want to go?'

Goopy didn't know what to say. 'We have come here to play for the king,' he told them finally.

That made the guards even more angry. They waved their spears and shouted, 'GET LOST!'

Goopy sneered. 'You wait and see. We will meet the king!' As soon as he said these words, their magic shoes took them right up to the king.

The king was asleep in his chamber. The queen was sitting next to him and gently fanning him. All of a sudden, Goopy and Bagha with his deafening drum arrived there without any warning. Their shoes had the power to take them anywhere, even through closed doors and windows.

Seeing them, the queen screamed and then fainted. The king, woken suddenly, jumped up from his bed and started running around the room like a madman. There was complete confusion throughout the palace. All the soldiers and guards came running, fully armed, ready to face any attack.

Goopy and Bagha had no idea what to do next. In their confusion, they forgot about their magical shoes. If they had only said, 'We want to go to this particular place', their shoes would have taken them there. Instead, they tried to run away.

Of course they could not run past the guards. As soon as they started running, poor Goopy and Bagha were caught and beaten up very badly—with sticks, shoes, whips, stones and whatever else the king's men could get hold of.

In the end, the king ordered, 'Take these rascals and keep them locked up for three days. After that, I will decide whether I want to chop off their heads or feed them to the dogs!'

Poor Goopy! Poor Bagha! They had only come to play music for the king and what trouble they were in! The guards tied up their hands and threw them into a dark dungeon. They took away Bagha's drum.

Goopy and Bagha's bodies ached so much that they couldn't move for a whole day. All they could do was groan in pain.

'Goopy,' said Bagha at last, 'first we got beaten up. Now we are going to die. I don't mind all that so much. What really upsets me is that I have lost my drum.'

But Goopy had recovered somewhat and was feeling far more clear-headed than Bagha. He patted Bagha on the back and said, 'Don't worry. We have lost our drum, but we still have our shoes and our magic bag. We were fools, that's why we got beaten up so badly. Anyway, we can still enjoy ourselves.'

'How?' asked Bagha, now a little pacified.

'First of all, we can have a good meal. Then we can think of how we can have some fun,' said Goopy.

Goopy put his hands into the bag the ghosts had given them and said, 'I want a pot of pulao.' As soon as he uttered the words, a wonderful aroma of pulao wafted through the air. Even kings had not tasted pulao which smelt so good. And the silver pot of pulao was so huge that Goopy could take it out of the bag only with great difficulty.

Then he ordered fried fish, chutney, yogurt and a whole lot of other delicacies. Slowly the room got filled with silver and golden dishes laden with wonderful food. The food was more than the two of them could eat, though they were ravenously hungry. As they ate, they could feel strength flow into their bodies, and their aches and pains seemed to reduce with each mouthful.

'Let's get out of here now,' said Bagha, sounding a little less mournful, 'before they feed us to the dogs.'

'Nonsense!' replied Goopy. 'With our magic shoes, we can escape from anything! Let's wait and see what happens.'

Bagha cheered up. He knew that Goopy was now going to do something entertaining.

The day went by. The king would pass judgement on them the following day.

That night Goopy put his hand into the bag and said, 'I want royal robes for both of us.' The robes he brought out from the bag were more beautiful than any clothes they had ever seen.

They put on these garments, tied their old clothes into a bundle, wore their shoes and said, 'We want to go out in the open and breathe the fresh air.'

As soon as they said these words, they reached an enormous field outside the king's palace. They hid their bundle of old clothes behind a bush and strolled up to the palace.

The royal guards saw them from a distance, and went and told the king that two mighty princes had come to visit him. Seeing their magnificent robes, the king also assumed that they were emperors of some land. He received Goopy and Bagha with great warmth and gave them one of the best rooms in the palace. Many attendants were asked to look after their needs.

After Goopy and Bagha had settled in their room, the king came to inquire after them. 'Which countries do you rule?' he asked them.

Goopy bowed and said 'My lord! How can we be kings? We are your servants.'

The king refused to believe him. 'Their speech is so refined! Their manners are so exquisite! Not only are they very rich emperors, they are also very courteous,' he thought.

The following morning, they were escorted to the king's court. The main matter of the day was deciding Goopy and Bagha's punishment.

Two guards were sent to fetch the prisoners. When they opened the door of the cell in the dungeon where they had been imprisoned, they found that it was empty!

There was much confusion. Everyone ran around, shouting at one another. The chief of guards called his men and gave them a severe scolding. 'It's not our fault,' pleaded the guards. 'We had locked the cell from outside and were standing at the door all this while. The two men must have been ghosts. How else could they have escaped?'

The king had decided to chop off the chief guard's head when he heard the prisoners were missing. When he heard this explanation, he changed his mind. 'You are right,' he said. 'The two of them must have been ghosts. My room was also locked. How could they have entered it? That too with such a big drum!'

'They were ghosts,' agreed everyone, and started trembling and sweating in terror.

Then someone thought of Bagha's drum. 'Your Highness!' he cried, 'the drum! The drum! Ghostly drums are dangerous things. You shouldn't keep the drum in the palace. We think it should be burnt immediately.'

'Ghostly drum in the palace! Burn it right now!' ordered the king.

As Bagha heard him, he started wailing loudly and tossing about on the floor.

Goopy didn't know what to do with Bagha. If he was crying at the prospect of his drum being burnt, what would he do when they actually set it on fire? Everyone would realize that it was his drum! Would they be able to get out alive?

Goopy felt like running away there and then. But escape wasn't possible because they had taken off their shoes before they sat down.

All the people in the court were alarmed to see Bagha behave like that. They thought that he had some strange incurable disease and was about to die.

The royal physician was sent for. He checked Bagha's pulse and shook his head solemnly. He gave him some bitter medicine to drink and rubbed some burning balm on his tummy. 'If this doesn't cure you, I will put some more balm on your back and sides,' he said.

Hearing that, Bagha stopped crying. People thought the royal physician had given Bagha a miraculous drug that had cured him instantly, and cheered the physician.

In the midst of the confusion everyone had forgotten about the drum. Bagha felt much better when he realized that, although the balm was burning his tummy. The king took him to his room and with great care made him lie down on his bed. Goopy sat down next to him and gently fanned him.

When everyone else had left the room, Goopy scolded Bagha. 'Why did you cry like that? We are now in trouble.'

'If I hadn't cried like that, they would have burnt my drum by now. This balm is burning a little, but my drum got saved!' replied Bagha.

The king went back to court. The chief of guards went up to him. 'Your Highness!' he whispered. 'I want to tell you something, if you will allow me.'

'What is it?' asked the king.

'It is about the man who was crying uncontrollably, and his friend. They are the two ghosts! I recognized them as soon as I saw them!'

'You are right!' said the king. 'I knew there was something suspicious about those characters. What do you think we should do now?'

Everyone in the court started discussing the matter. Someone said, 'Let's call the witch doctor. He will chase them away.'

'What if the witch doctor is not able to drive them away? They can cause us great harm. Why don't we burn them while they are asleep?' suggested someone else.

Everyone liked the idea. But there was one problem. If they tried burning the ghosts, the palace might also catch fire. After much thought, it was decided that they would ask the two of them to stay in the king's country house. Even if the country house got burnt down, there wouldn't be much harm done.

'Let's keep the drum there as well,' said the king. 'When we set fire to the country house, we will get rid of the two ghosts along with their drum!'

Goopy and Bagha were very happy when they learnt that they were going to stay in the country house. They didn't know that this was a plot to kill them and thought they would be able to stay there in comfort and practise their music in solitude.

They moved to the new house the following day. The house was very peaceful. It was made of wood, and beautifully designed. Bagha got better soon after they shifted there.

As soon as he recovered, Goopy wanted to leave. 'Why should we stay here any longer?' he said. 'Let's get going.'

But Bagha was reluctant to go. 'Let's spend some more time here,' he said. 'We won't ever get such a beautiful place to live in. If only I had my drum…' He wandered off sadly to look around the house.

Goopy sat in the garden, humming to himself. All of a sudden, he heard Bagha shouting like a madman. Goopy couldn't make out what he was saying, except the words 'Goopy! Goopy!'

Goopy ran indoors. Bagha was holding his drum above his head, dancing and shouting in joy. For about half an hour he babbled continuously and was incapable of standing still. After that, he calmed down a little.

'I found my drum in that little room!' he said to Goopy and danced a bit more. Then he said, 'Goopy! I have got my drum back after such a long time. Please sing a little. I'll play it along with you.'

'Not now,' said Goopy. 'I'm very hungry, and the king has organized a big feast for us. After dinner we can sit outside and sing and play to our hearts' content.'

The king had asked the chief of guards to arrange for a big feast in the country house that evening. About fifty guests had been invited. The plan was that after the feast, when Goopy and Bagha fell asleep, they would set fire to the house. The two would be trapped inside.

The feast was a success, but Goopy and Bagha were waiting for the guests to go, so that they could play music together. The chief of guards was waiting for Goopy and Bagha to fall asleep so that the house could be set on fire. He kept pestering them to go to bed and he made it very clear to them that he would not leave till they were asleep. When Goopy and Bagha saw there was no way out, they went to bed and started snoring.

A little while later, the house was quiet again. Goopy and Bagha waited a bit more, just to make sure that no one was around. Then they came out to the veranda and started playing music. They were so absorbed in what they were doing that they did not notice what was happening in the house behind them.

After they had gone to bed, the chief of guards had told his men to set fire to each and every door. 'Don't leave till you see the door burning,' he had said. And he himself had set the staircase on fire. Soon the wooden house was burning merrily. 'It's time we left,' thought the chief of guards.

Just then Goopy started singing and Bagha began playing his drum. All the guards suddenly found they could not move. In increasing panic, they stood like statues, rolling their eyes helplessly. And everyone got burnt.

Goopy and Bagha noticed the fire in the nick of time. They took their bag and Bagha's drum, and escaped with the help of their shoes.

The chief of guards got killed in the fire. Most of his men also died. The few who were still alive went to the king and told him a curious tale. They told him about the strange music that they had heard while the house was getting burnt down. They described how the two ghosts had flown in the air and vanished from sight.

You can't imagine how much all this scared the king! He quickly ran into his room, bolted the door and lay in bed covered with blankets. He didn't venture out for an entire month!

In their hurry to escape from the fire, Goopy and Bagha had said the first thing which came to their heads, which was: 'To the forest.' Instantly they reached a forest, which looked familiar.

'Isn't this where we met?' asked Bagha.

'Yes!' Goopy agreed.

'Since we have reached this special place, don't you think we should spend some time here playing music?' asked Bagha.

'Why not?' said Goopy. 'Let's start right away.'

So the two of them started singing and playing the drum with great zest.

Meanwhile, drama had been unfolding in the neighbouring kingdom of Halla. A band of robbers had looted the king's treasury, captured his two young sons and were running away. The king's soldiers chased them, but the robbers escaped into the safety of the forest.

As the robbers were congratulating themselves on their escape, Goopy and Bagha started playing and singing. Hearing their song, the robbers (and their captives) were frozen into immobility. Goopy and Bagha sang and played through the night, unaware that they had an audience. And their listeners stood like statues all night.

Early in the morning, just as the music stopped, the king of Halla and his soldiers reached the forest and captured the dazed robbers very easily.

The two princes told the king the tale of the music which had made the robbers incapable of running away. The soldiers went to look for the musicians and found them sleeping.

The king treated Goopy and Bagha with great respect. 'Father, we have not heard such wonderful music before. Let's take them along with us,' pleaded his sons.

The king happily agreed. 'Come with us. I'll pay you a salary of five hundred rupees,' he said to them.

Goopy and Bagha were very happy with the offer. But they requested the king to give them two days' time. Since they were so close to their homes, they wanted to visit their parents. 'We will meet them and come to your kingdom,' they promised.

'We will rest for two days in the forest,' said the king. 'Go and visit your parents. You will find us here.'

Goopy's parents had been feeling very sad after throwing him out of their house. They were overjoyed to see him again.

But Bagha was not so lucky. His father and mother had both died soon after he had left the village. When the people of his village saw him approaching, with the drum on his head, they said, 'He has come to trouble us again! Beat the rascal!'

'I have only come here to visit my parents,' pleaded Bagha. 'I'll go away after two days. And I promise not to play my drum.'

No one listened to him. They came charging at him with big sticks. Poor Bagha had to run for his life. But as he was running, he slipped and fell. He broke his leg and cracked his skull.

Goopy was standing at his door, talking to his father, when he saw Bagha coming towards him. He was limping, and his clothes were torn and covered with blood.

Goopy ran up to Bagha. 'Why are you in this state, my friend?' he said.

Even in his pain, Bagha smiled at Goopy. 'I had a narrow escape,' he said. 'The idiots nearly broke my drum!'

Bagha stayed at Goopy's house for two days. Goopy and his parents good took care of him. While bidding his family farewell, Goopy told them to be ready to move to Halla.

'I'll come and take you with me when I get leave,' he said to them.

A few months went by. Goopy and Bagha were happily settled in the palace of the king of Halla. Their fame had spread far and wide. People said they were the greatest musicians on earth. The king loved them. He couldn't do without listening to their music at least once every day. He would confide all his joys and sorrows to them.

One day Goopy noticed that the king looked very sad and worried. When asked, he told Goopy what was bothering him. 'I'm in great trouble, Goopy,' he said. 'The king of Shundi wants to take over my kingdom. He will attack us any day.'

The king of Shundi was the one who had wanted to burn Goopy and Bagha. Goopy thought for a while and got a brilliant idea. 'Your Highness,' he said, 'please don't worry about this. Just command me and I will deal with this problem.'

The king smiled sadly. 'You are a musician,' he said. 'What do you know about war? The king of Shundi has a huge army. I'll be quite helpless when it arrives.'

'If you permit me, I can at least try,' said Goopy. 'There's no harm in trying.'

'Go ahead and do what you want,' said the king.

Goopy ran to discuss the matter with Bagha. They thought hard and talked longer as they decided on their plan of action. Bagha was also very enthusiastic about Goopy's idea. 'We have to save the king,' he said. 'My only fear is that when we have to escape, we might forget our magic shoes and get badly bashed up. Do you remember the way I got hammered by the fools of our village? It wouldn't have happened if I had remembered the shoes.'

Goopy assured Bagha that it wouldn't happen again.

The following night they went to Shundi and roamed around the palace collecting information. They continued doing this for a few nights. The arrangements made for the war were very extensive. The king of Halla didn't have a chance against the mighty army of Shundi. In case any further aid was needed, the people of Shundi were also offering prayers to the gods in the temple every day. This would continue for ten days, after which they would set out to capture Halla. Goopy and Bagha noted all these details.

Then came the next stage in their plan. One night, they found themselves a secluded room in the palace in Shundi, locked the door securely and spoke to the bag the ghosts had given them. 'We want sweets of the most wonderful kind. They should look delicious beyond compare,' they said.

The sweets that appeared in the bag were delicious beyond description. No one had ever seen or tasted anything like them! Goopy and Bagha took the sweets and flew to the spire of the temple, where they sat waiting in the darkness.

The temple and the courtyard in front were packed with people. There was a lot of commotion. Prayers were being chanted and people were busy talking to one another. The courtyard was dark and smoky.

Goopy and Bagha dropped the pots of sweets, and they fell down to the courtyard, over the heads of the people below. Then they clung to the spire and watched the fun.

As the sweets fell, everyone became silent. Many in the crowd jumped in fright. Others began screaming and running around. Some people looked up to see where they had come from, but Goopy and Bagha were safely hidden in the darkness. A few of the braver ones picked up the sweets, held them against the light and examined them closely.

One man shut his eyes and, with great courage, put a sweet in his mouth. When he tasted the delicious confection, he squealed in joy and amazement. As everyone around him watched, he grabbed another and yet another, making happy sounds as he ate. Some more people tried the sweets, and soon everyone in the courtyard was fighting over them.

A few of the men ran to the king. 'Your Highness,' they said, 'the gods are so pleased with us that they have showered us with sweets which are delicious beyond description!'

The king took a deep breath and hurried towards the temple.

But alas! All the sweets had been eaten up. There wasn't even a crumb left for the king to taste. He was furious. 'This is unpardonable!' he said. 'I prayed to the gods and you ate up all their gifts! You didn't leave even the tiniest morsel for me! I will hang the lot of you!'

Everyone trembled in fear. 'Please, Your Highness!' they begged him. 'They were over before we even realized it. Please forgive us. We won't touch the sweets tomorrow. We will keep them all for you.'

'All right,' agreed the king, 'but don't you dare forget!'

The next day the king reached the temple early in the evening. He sat in the courtyard, gazing at the sky. Everyone else stood some distance away from him. They were a little scared, but also eager to watch the fun.

The ceremonies in the temple that evening were a hundred times more elaborate than on other days. Everyone thought that the gods would be so pleased that they would shower even better sweets on the king.

Late in the evening, Goopy and Bagha went up to the spire dressed in shiny robes. They had adorned themselves with crowns, bangles, necklaces and earrings. They carried pots of sweets that were even more wonderful than the ones they had thrown down the previous day.

The courtyard was smoky, so nobody could see anything. But they all kept staring up nevertheless.

Goopy and Bagha dropped all the pots of sweets on the king's head. At first, the king let out a scream of surprise and pain. Then he leapt up, and put one sweet in his mouth, and then another, and began dancing with joy!

Goopy and Bagha floated down from the spire and stood before the king.

'The gods have come! The gods have come!' shouted everybody and scrambled to kneel down and pray. The king lay flat on his tummy, banging his head on the ground in reverence.

'Your Highness,' said Goopy, 'I am very pleased with your devotion. Come! Let me embrace you!'

The king's joy knew no bounds when he heard this. After all, how many people are lucky enough to be hugged by a god?

Goopy embraced the king amidst much cheering. Then he said, 'Come home with us.'

The crowds parted in wonder as Goopy and Bagha took the king by both arms and rose slowly into the sky.

The people in the courtyard stared into the sky for a long time after the three of them vanished. When their king didn't return, they went and told everyone in the kingdom about the wonderful sight that they had seen. 'The king went straight to heaven. Two gods had come to fetch him,' they said.

The king had fainted in Goopy's arms as they flew. They took him back to the palace in Halla, and waited patiently for him to open his eyes.

The king regained consciousness early the following morning. The first sight that met his eyes was the two ghosts sitting beside him. Trembling with fear, he fell off the bed and at their feet. 'Please don't eat me,' he begged them. 'I will sacrifice two hundred buffaloes for you.'

'Your Highness!' said Goopy. 'Neither are we ghosts, nor are we going to eat you.'

This did not pacify the king. He sat in one corner, hiding his face and trembling fearfully.

Goopy and Bagha went to the king of Halla. 'We have captured and brought the king of Shundi for you,' they said. 'Command us what to do next.'

'Bring him here!' ordered the king.

When the king of Shundi met the king of Halla, he realized that he had been tricked and captured by his enemy. He knew that instead of getting the kingdom of Halla, he would probably be killed.

But the king of Halla didn't kill him. He only took away his kingdom. Then he called Goopy and Bagha, thanked them, gave them half of Shundi to rule and got them married to his two daughters.

Goopy and Bagha were so happy with the way things had turned out that they started devoting even more time to music. Goopy's parents were very proud of their son!

KENARAM BECHARAM

Characters

Kenaram, the servant

Becharam, the master

An angel in disguise

Scene I

Kenaram enters the room, darning a shirt.

KENARAM: Oh, no! It's torn again! This shirt tears every time I touch it! How on earth am I going to repair it again? What a miserly master I have! I've seen him wearing this torn shirt for the last three years. I wonder how much longer he'll use it. I wouldn't mind it so much if he gave me enough to eat. But what food! He eats a bit of rice in the morning. I get to drink the starch left behind. At night, he licks the bottom of the vessel of rice and I can only sniff it! And his sense of hearing is terrific! He can't hear anything you tell him! The other day, the landlord came to ask for money. 'You owe me a lot of money. Pay up now,' he said. ' So we are invited to your house for dinner tonight?' asked my master. The landlord said, 'You have to settle the dues right now.' And my master said, 'Can I bring my servant along?' The poor landlord didn't know what to do! He went back in a huff! To get rich, one must behave like my master, I suppose. By living with him, I've learnt how to get rich.

Though *getting* rich here is impossible! My master had made many promises when I started working for him. But he hasn't paid me anything over the last three years. If he doesn't pay my salary today, I'm going to leave, so there!

Kenaram exits.

Becharam enters.

BECHARAM: I just gave him my shirt to repair, and what a lot the stupid fellow had to say! I heard it all. The idiot thinks I am deaf. If he had ears as sharp as mine, he wouldn't be working for me. Just by listening at the door, I can make out how many people there are in the house, how many of them are asleep and how many awake. I can tell if there are cockroaches in a cupboard. My ears tell me everything! Of course I can hear. I can hear very well, thank you! But not hearing also has its advantages. By simply pretending to be deaf, I don't need to pay my landlord or my servant…

Kenaram enters.

KENARAM *in a loud voice*: Master! I want my salary for the last three years. If you don't pay me, I'll leave right now!

BECHARAM: The postman? A letter? Show me.

KENARAM *aside*: This is what he does every time. But this time I've come prepared. I've written it all down.

To Becharam: Yes, a letter. Here it is.

BECHARAM *reading aloud:* Respected Sir, I know you can't hear very well. But you can read. Please pay my salary for the last three years. I wish to leave. Yours truly, Kenaram.

To Kenaram: You're right. I have to pay your salary. The amount wasn't decided when you joined. You haven't worked well either. You don't deserve more than three paise for the last three years! Here is your money. Take it!

Scene II

Kenaram enters.

KENARAM: I am rich at last. Three paise for the last three years!

One, two, three, one, two, three, one, two, three…

He puts the money into his pocket. An angel in disguise enters.

ANGEL: You seem to be very pleased about something.

KENARAM: Who are you, small man? Let me wear my glasses and look at you properly.

ANGEL: Do you have weak eyes?

KENARAM: Oh, no! I have just become very rich. I find it difficult to see lesser people.

ANGEL: Is that so? How did you suddenly become so rich?

KENARAM: I just got my salary for the last three years. O-n-e t-w-o t-h-r-e-e.

He takes out the three paise.

ANGEL: So much money! What will you do with it? Give me some.

KENARAM: Do you want the money? It's yours. I can work hard and earn again.

He gives the money to the angel.

ANGEL: You are a good man with a kind heart. I am actually an angel from heaven. I reward all the good people I meet. I am very pleased with you. Tell me what you want. It will be yours.

KENARAM: Are you an angel? I have been very rude to you.

ANGEL: No, you haven't. Tell me what your heart desires.

KENARAM: If you really want to give me something, give me a trumpet that will make people dance every time I blow it.

ANGEL *taking a trumpet out of his bag*: Here it is.

KENARAM: Thank you. I hope I don't have to dance when I hear it.

ANGEL: No, you don't. Go and have fun.

Kenaram starts blowing the trumpet.

ANGEL: Just wait till I leave! I don't want to dance!

Scene III

Becharam enters.

BECHARAM: I had left it behind this bush when the police were after me. They had nearly caught me. I threw the bag of money here. Hope I can find it. What thorns! Ah! I got it!

Scene IV

Kenaram enters.

KENARAM *to himself*: Ah! Here is Becharam Babu! What is he doing behind the bushes? Let me blow my trumpet once.

He blows the trumpet.

BECHARAM *dancing helplessly*: What is this? Ooh! Aah! What are you . . . Ooh! Why are you . . . Ouch! All my clothes will tear!

KENARAM: I am your humble servant. You have just paid me my salary. I was playing this to show you my gratitude.

He blows the trumpet again with great enthusiasm.

BECHARAM *still dancing*: Please Kenaram! Have pity on me! What is this trumpet? Why do I dance every time I hear it? Take all this money. Stop playing.

He gives Kenaram the bag of money.

KENARAM: I'll stop blowing the trumpet right now. I have a very good master. I have no wish to trouble him. But I see that the sound of my trumpet has cured your ears. Please tell me if your ears trouble you again. I'll come and blow my trumpet.

Kenaram departs after bidding Becharam farewell.

BECHARAM: Rascal! Scoundrel! Cheat! Thug! Just wait and see! Police! Police! I've just been robbed!

Scene V

Becharam enters the court in a purposeful manner.

BECHARAM: I have been robbed! What will I do now?

He cries noisily.

JUDGE: What is the matter? What has happened to you?

BECHARAM *showing the scratches on his body made by the thorns*: I have been robbed. My former servant beat me up and took all my money.

Becharam cries some more.

I fed him and looked after him for the last three years. This is what I get in return! He roams around with a trumpet. Send someone after him. He will recognize him when he sees the trumpet.

JUDGE: I'll send four men after him right away.

Scene VI

Four men drag Kenaram into the court.

BECHARAM: This is the rascal! Kenaram has stolen all the money I had! Beat him up!

JUDGE: Silence!

To Kenaram: Have you beaten him up and stolen all his money?

KENARAM: No, sir. He has given this money to me as a reward for playing music. I swear it.

JUDGE: Someone who has rewarded you for playing music wouldn't look so unhappy. Besides, there are scratches on his body. Thus it is proved that you beat him and stole his money. You are a robber. We punish robbers by hanging them. Before we hang you, I want to know if you have a last wish.

KENARAM: No, sir. I have no wishes. I only want to blow my trumpet one last time.

BECHARAM: Don't listen to him sir. Please don't allow him to blow his trumpet.

JUDGE *to Becharam*: Shut up!

To Kenaram: Go ahead. Blow it.

Kenaram starts blowing his trumpet with gusto. Everyone in the court, from the peon to the judge, starts dancing.

JUDGE *panting and out of breath*: Stop it! I tell you stop it! I'll let you off. I give the verdict that you are innocent. My god! What a trumpet!

KENARAM *saluting the judge*: Sir, please ask Becharam Babu to relate what actually happened. Or else I'll start playing music again.

JUDGE *to Becharam*: Tell me the truth. I want to know exactly what happened.

BECHARAM: Please don't blow the trumpet again, I beg you. I gave that money to Kenaram.

JUDGE: Where did you get so much money from?

KENARAM: Should I blow it again?

BECHARAM: No, no. I'll tell you everything. I stole that money last night.

KENARAM: What did I tell you, sir?

JUDGE: Whip the rascal twenty-five times and lock him up!

DUKHIRAM

Dukhiram means 'the unlucky one'. Dukhiram's real name was far nicer, but unfortunately I have forgotten what it was.

Dukhiram was born in a poor family. When he was just two years old, both his parents died. His uncle Keshto was his only living relative. At that time, Dukhiram did not know about his uncle's existence. Keshto did not bother to find out how his nephew was. Dukhiram's neighbours took pity on him and brought him up, and it was they who gave him this name.

Dukhiram's foster parents were very kind, but they were very poor. He barely got to eat two square meals a day. Who could afford to send him to school? He spent his time reading other children's torn and discarded books and doing odd jobs for people in his neighbourhood. He grew up to be a very clever boy nevertheless.

When Dukhiram was a young man, he heard that he had an uncle called Keshto. He decided that he would find his uncle and pay him a visit. After all, his foster parents had taken care of him for many years, and it was time that his only surviving relative did something. After asking many people, he managed to find out where his uncle lived.

When Dukhiram arrived and introduced himself, Keshto was less than delighted. Hoping to make him go away, Keshto said, 'Oh, Dukhiram, I would love to have you stay here! But as you can see, we don't live in comfort. We eat only once in two months. We ate yesterday. We'll have our next meal two months later!'

'Please don't worry, uncle,' said Dukhiram. 'I'll eat whenever you all eat.'

Keshto couldn't think of anything to say to that. So Dukhiram started living with his uncle and his cousin Hari that very day.

Keshto and Hari didn't eat anything the whole day. So Dukhiram didn't get anything to eat either. But Dukhiram was used to starving for much longer, and his hunger did not affect him much.

In the evening, he said to Keshto, 'Uncle, I'm very sleepy. I want to go to bed. Where should I sleep?'

Keshto was very happy to hear that. He spread a mat on the floor. Dukhiram lay down quietly.

A short while later, Keshto and Hari came and lay down beside him. The light was turned off. There was silence, except for the steady sound of breathing.

Actually, no one was asleep. Keshto lay there wondering when Dukhiram would fall asleep. And Dukhiram was waiting to see what his uncle would do next. Hari was just feeling hungry. After a while, Hari started snoring.

Dukhiram heard a rustling sound in the darkness, and knew that his uncle had got up and tiptoed out. There was the sound of the kitchen door being closed quietly. Then he heard the clang of pots and pans, the sound of running water and the hiss of the stove.

Dukhiram got up and peeped through a hole in the kitchen door. His uncle was busy cooking *payas*, with rice, thickened milk and sugar.

Dukhiram watched his uncle for some time, and then he went back to bed. At intervals, he got up to see whether the *payas* was done.

At last, when the he saw that the *payas* was ready, Dukhiram sat up in bed and started howling loudly.

Keshto quickly came from the kitchen and asked, 'What is the matter, Dukhiram?'

'When you were in the kitchen, someone was watching you through a hole in the door,' said Dukhiram.

That someone was actually Dukhiram himself, but his uncle thought that it was a thief. So he took a stick and ran into the forest at the back of the house to chase the thief!

Dukhiram woke Hari up and said, 'Get up, cousin! Your father has just rushed off somewhere with a stick in his hand!'

Poor Hari was very worried when he heard that. Since his father had taken a stick, he thought that his father must have gone somewhere quite far. His sister lived three miles away. Maybe she had suddenly fallen ill and hearing this, his father had gone to visit her. So Hari got up and went off to his sister's house.

A little while later Keshto returned. He hadn't caught the thief. But he had brushed against some poison ivy in the woods and he was itching all over. When he found Hari missing, he asked Dukhiram where he was.

Dukhiram told him the truth. 'Uncle, after you went away, the man who was peeping through the hole in the door woke Hari up and said something to him. And Hari went off at once,' he said.

Keshto thought that Hari must have taken advantage of his absence to go and play cards with some unruly boy in the neighbourhood. He felt really angry with Hari and the unruly boy, whoever he was. So he went off again with the stick, this time to find the mischievous lads and punish them.

Dukhiram saw that both his uncle and his cousin would be away for some time. He tiptoed into the kitchen and gently removed the lid from the pot of *payas*. He was ravenous and his uncle had cooked the *payas* really well. Very soon the pot was empty.

Dukhiram went back to his mat and fell asleep contented.

Hari reached his sister's house and saw that she was well. His sister refused to let him return home that night as it was very late.

Keshto searched all over the town for his son, but was unable to find him. He came home fuming. He was so angry and itching all over so badly that he couldn't sleep. When Hari returned home early in the morning, Keshto gave him a sound thrashing.

When Keshto went into the kitchen later in the morning, he found that the pot containing the *payas* was empty! Keshto was no fool, and he understood at once what had happened. He also noticed that Dukhiram was giving him sidelong glances and smiling to himself. Keshto had no doubt that the culprit was Dukhiram.

Father and son went to the king to complain. The king sent for Dukhiram and asked him, 'Why did you do this? Why did you steal their *payas*? Why did you give them so much trouble by lying to them?'

With folded hands, Dukhiram said, 'Please, Your Highness! They told me that they eat once in two months. They said they ate the day before yesterday. So why did they cook *payas* yesterday? You should ask them that. You are saying that I troubled them, but I only told them the truth. If they got so troubled hearing the truth, it is their fault, not mine!'

The king was very amused to hear the whole story. The case was dismissed.

Seeing that Dukhiram was such a clever fellow, the king gave him a job. Dukhiram was very good at his work. Within a year he got promoted and became a deputy minister. People knew that he would be made a minister as soon as there was a vacancy.

The chief minister was an unpleasant man. He was very jealous of Dukhiram's success. He would spend hours thinking of how he could land the young man in trouble.

The minister had a friend called Sulakshan, who was a merchant. Sulakshan owned a wonderful horse, which could talk like a human being and fly like a bird! It had other talents: it could cover large distances in minutes, and it could predict the future. The minister had been eyeing the horse for a long time, but Sulakshan had no desire to part with it.

Sulakshan also possessed a wondrous mango seed, which he had brought back from his travels in distant lands. As soon as the seed was planted, a sapling would appear and then grow rapidly into a tree. It would bear mangoes, which would ripen instantly and would be ready to eat! Best of all, one could take the seed out from beneath the tree and use it again.

The minister won over the merchant's servant with a large bribe. He asked the servant to boil the mango seed secretly.

One day the minister said to Sulakshan, 'My friend, I've heard that you have brought back a magical mango seed from your travels.'

'Yes,' said Sulakshan eagerly. 'It grows into a tree as soon as you plant it. Then it bears mangoes, which ripen instantly!'

The minister turned up his nose and said, 'I don't believe you.'

'Let's have a bet,' said Sulakshan. 'What will you give me if I am proved to be correct?'

'You can come to my house tomorrow. The first thing that you touch will be yours,' said the minister. 'And what will I get if I am right?'

Sulakshan replied, 'Then you can come to my house tomorrow and take whatever you first lay your hands on.'

It was decided that the minister would be invited to the merchant's house for dinner and the mango seed would be put to test. Since the seed had been boiled, you can guess what the result of the test was. Sulakshan realized that he had been tricked and the minister would now take his flying horse.

He thought the matter over for a long time. He racked his brains, but he couldn't find a solution to his problem. So finally, he went to Dukhiram. He wept and told Dukhiram what had happened.

Dukhiram pondered for some time and then told Sulakshan what he should do. The merchant, now much relieved, came home, tied the door of his horse's stable with a rope and slept in peace.

The next day, the minister arrived at Sulakshan's house at the crack of dawn. 'My friend! My friend!' he called several times, for the household was still asleep.

Sulakshan woke up and welcomed him. The minister didn't want to waste any time chatting. 'What about your promise?' he asked as soon as he entered the house.

'I'm ready,' replied Sulakshan. 'You can touch anything you want. It will be yours.'

The minister went straight towards the stable and the merchant followed him.

The door of the stable was secured with a rope. With one tug, the minister untied the rope.

'What have you done, my friend!' cried Sulakshan. 'Why should a great man like you want to possess a rope like this? I would have been happy if you had touched something more expensive. But yes, of course, you can have the rope.'

The minister felt very foolish. He had not expected to be defeated so easily. He didn't answer, and went away, muttering angrily to himself.

On his way home, the minister thought about the matter. He decided that the trick played on him must have been the deputy minister's idea. His suspicions were confirmed when he heard that Sulakshan had visited Dukhiram the previous night.

The next afternoon, when the king was asleep, the minister went to his palace. He stood in front of the king, with his hands folded. The king woke up and asked, 'What is the matter?'

'Your Highness!' the minister replied. 'Sulakshan the merchant possesses a flying horse, but Your Majesty has none.'

The king said, 'Is that so? I want that horse!'

With tears in his eyes, the minister pleaded, 'I try to do what is best for you, but the deputy minister always comes in the way.'

'Why do you say that?' asked the king.

'I tried to get the flying horse for you. But Dukhiram didn't allow Sulakshan to give me the horse,' the minister said.

Kings in those days were very moody people. Small things could make them extremely happy or really angry. When they rewarded people, they would give them half their kingdom. And when they punished someone, they would order that his head be chopped off! The king had been very pleased with Dukhiram so far. That is why he had made him the deputy minister. But when he heard the chief minister's complaints, he was so enraged that he ordered his men to bring Dukhiram with his hands and feet tied.

Poor Dukhiram had no idea what had happened. He was blissfully asleep when all of a sudden the king's men barged into his house, tied him up and carried him away. He was put into a sack. The king then asked his guards to throw the sack into the sea with a heavy stone tied to its end.

Everyone loved Dukhiram. When they heard about his punishment they were all very unhappy. On the way, the guards discussed the matter and decided that they would never throw a good man like Dukhiram into the sea.

They took him instead to a forest by the sea and freed him. They gave him the hangman's axe they were carrying (to kill him in case he got away) and a piece of cloth and said, 'Dear deputy minister, we have nothing else to offer you. You can sell wood in the forest and earn a living. But we beg you, please don't come back. If the king sees you, he will spare neither you nor us.'

Thus Dukhiram became a woodcutter. He let his hair and beard grow. He discarded his old clothes and wore the piece of cloth the guards had given him. His skin grew dark because he was out in the sun all day. He didn't get enough to eat and he grew quite thin. It was now difficult to recognize him. Days went by and Dukhiram lived in hardship.

Early one morning, when Dukhiram set off to cut wood, he saw an ancient-looking woman asleep beside a stream. Dukhiram had never seen anyone so old. He was about to walk by when he saw a poisonous snake slithering up to her. At once Dukhiram chopped the snake up into pieces with his axe and threw the pieces into the stream. As the pieces fell into the stream, all the water in it started boiling. The old woman woke up with a start when she heard the sound of boiling water.

The old woman was so surprised to see Dukhiram that she stared at him for some time. Then she asked him, 'Who are you, my son?'

Dukhiram told her his name.

'What do you want?' the old woman asked

'I don't want anything,' replied Dukhiram. 'What is an old person like you doing in the forest? It's teeming with wild animals. Get away from here quickly.'

'You saved my life. I can't go away without giving you something,' insisted the old woman.

But Dukhiram would not take anything, so the old woman prepared to leave. But just before she went, she whispered, 'I'll grant you a boon. You will get whatever you wish for.'

Dukhiram had walked away in the other direction by this time. He did not hear what the old woman had said.

Talking to the old woman had made Dukhiram late. He had to cut wood and sell it in the market. Only then would he get something to eat. He felt so troubled thinking about it that he didn't look where he was going. A small tree had fallen on the way and he stumbled on it and fell. He was already sad. This accident made him very angry. 'I wish there were no trees here,' he said.

As soon as he said that, all the trees there disappeared! What was once a dense forest became an open field!

What bad luck! Where would he now get wood from and what would he eat? Dukhiram was too bewildered by what had happened to connect it to what he had said. He had no idea why the forest had disappeared. He kept walking, but he could see no trees anywhere.

It was quite late in the morning by now, and Dukhiram was very hungry. He found it difficult to walk with such a heavy axe in his hand. After all, it was the hangman's axe and twice as heavy as ordinary axes. Dukhiram was feeling so weak that the axe seemed to be ten times heavier than usual. Finally, Dukhiram flung it away and said, 'I can't carry it any more. I wish this axe had legs. Then it could walk along with me!'

The axe did just that! Suddenly, the axe had legs, which were exactly like those of a spider. And the axe started following him on its little legs.

Dukhiram felt dizzy when he saw what was happening. He kept walking mechanically, while his head seethed with amazement at the miraculous things which were happening to him.

In a daze, Dukhiram walked and walked, until he reached the town where he had grown up. He walked on until he reached the marketplace. His faithful axe still followed him, walking confidently as though it had been walking all its life!

If you saw an axe walking by with long strides, what would you do? If such an axe reached the marketplace, what would all the people there do?

The first shop in the market was the milkman's shop. A rich man's servant had come there to buy butter. The servant had just given the milkman a bowl to put the butter in and was about to light his cigarette when he suddenly saw Dukhiram's axe walking up to him! He gave a loud scream, leaped into the air and fell on top of the milkman. The milkman, who had also just seen the axe, pushed him away in panic into the pot containing butter. He then ran into his shop and shut the door. A little while later, when he saw that the axe was quite harmless, the milkman opened

the door. Then the servant and the milkman followed the axe to watch the fun.

No one bought anything at the market that day. All the servants and householders who had come to do their shopping abandoned their errands and followed the axe. The shopkeepers for once had no interest in selling, but shut their shops and trailed after the axe. Even the policemen and the guards did the same.

When people came to look for their missing servants, they also stayed back to watch the axe. Soon almost all the people in the kingdom had collected there. Dukhiram's uncle Keshto and his cousin Hari were among the people assembled.

At first, Keshto and Hari were busy watching the axe. But after a while they noticed the man that it was following.

As soon as their eyes fell on Dukhiram, their hearts started beating louder. In spite of his beard and ragged appearance, they knew it was Dukhiram. They quickly went to the chief minister and informed him that Dukhiram had returned.

The minister ran to the king. 'Your Highness! Have you ever heard of an axe walking?' he said. 'Dukhiram must have learnt black magic and come here with some evil purpose.'

'You are right!' said the king. 'Send ten soldiers to tie up Dukhiram and bring him here!'

And ten men, so big and strong that they looked like demons, set out to fetch Dukhiram, accompanied by the minister.

Meanwhile, people in the market hadn't paid much attention to Dukhiram. After watching the axe for many hours, someone decided that they should take it to the king. And that was when they discovered that the axe was unbelievably strong! First one man tried to pull it, then a few, then some ten men—but with no effect. Finally, all the men in the market tied a rope around the axe and pulled with ALL their strength. But they could not drag the axe in the direction they wanted it to go! Instead, the axe dragged the men with it for over half a mile!

At that point, the king's men appeared. 'Tie him up tightly!' the minister ordered them, pointing towards Dukhiram.

Dukhiram was no longer surprised by the happenings of that day. He had been silently watching events unfold and wondering what would happen next. But when the men started to tie him up, he was very saddened. He told the minister, 'It's easy to trouble others. What would you do if something like this happened to you?'

Instantly four of the king's men abandoned Dukhiram and moved to the minister. They threw him down and started tying him up!

At first, the minister was too surprised to react. Then he became furious and started yelling at them, but the men paid no attention to his protests and proceeded with their work.

The minister was so livid that he couldn't speak any more. His eyes nearly popped out. The veins on his neck swelled up, and he was frothing at the mouth.

After the men had tied the minister up, they tested to see if they had tied him as securely as they had tied Dukhiram. Satisfied with their work, the men flung Dukhiram and the minister over their shoulders and took them to the king. The people in the market, who had been watching everything with astonishment, followed them.

When all these people reached the king's palace, the king was surprised, but not too angry. He freed the minister with his own hands. Then the two of them sat down to pass judgement on Dukhiram and the four soldiers who had tied up the minister. It was easy enough to decide what to do with the soldiers—they would be hanged. But it took more time to decide what to do with Dukhiram, as he had managed to escape his punishment the previous time. They argued until it was lunchtime, and then, because they were hungry, they decided to postpone the sentence until after they had eaten.

Most of the spectators, however, found the whole business so exciting that they stayed back to watch even after the king and minister had left.

Poor Dukhiram lay on the floor, still tied up and surrounded on all sides by guards. How can I describe how miserable he felt? He did not think so much about his other woes, but his hunger was unbearable and would not go away.

Dukhiram thought of all the delicious things the king and minister were eating. 'If only someone could get the same food for me,' he thought to himself.

The king washed his hands and sat down to eat. The minister sat by him. The golden plates in front of them had a hundred courses on them. The wonderful aromas mingled and made one's mouth water.

The king reached out to pick up the first mouthful. Just then his plate with all the food on it vanished into thin air! The same thing happened to the minister's plate.

As Dukhiram lay sadly, the two plates laden with food appeared in front of him. Dukhiram was beyond surprise, but he felt sad that he could not eat. 'If only my hands and feet were not tied up,' he thought.

Immediately, the ropes binding him untied themselves and slid off. With one leap Dukhiram got up and, using both his hands, started gobbling up the pulao, mutton, *payas*, sweets and all the other delicacies in front of him.

The guards were completely dumbfounded by what they saw. One of them soon came back to his senses and said, 'Catch him quickly before he runs away!'

Another guard said, 'How can he run away? There are so many of us surrounding him. There is so much food in front of him. Let him eat in peace.'

Dukhiram was so grateful at this kindness that he said, 'I want all of you to become kings!'

In the twinkling of an eye, one thousand thrones, each exactly like the king's throne, appeared in the room! The guards and spectators too were magically garbed in princely robes. As they gawked in amazement, they found their feet guiding them inexorably to the thrones, where they sat down in bafflement.

The king came back to the court, grumpy and hungry (he had to eat whatever leftovers there were in the royal kitchen). He saw that there were a thousand more kings seated all around his throne. They all said to him with one voice, 'Please, Your Highness! Release this man.'

What could the king do? He could hardly say no to so many kings.

So Dukhiram was set free.

At this point, the minister appeared. He was totally dumbfounded to see so many kings. Wherever he looked, he saw a king, and he had to salute each of them. He had got very little food at lunch. After saluting one thousand and one kings, he started feeling hungry again.

When he heard about Dukhiram, the minister got very upset. With folded hands, he pleaded with all the kings, 'Your Royal Highnesses! Do reconsider your judgement. If you let this rascal go, you don't know how much harm he can cause.'

One of the kings replied, 'What harm has he done? I was your sweeper. He has made me a king and you have saluted me.'

The minister looked closely and saw that the king who was speaking to him was actually his sweeper! Slowly he and the king realized that of the kings seated there, some were guards, some messengers, some shopkeepers and some beggars!

The king and the minister felt so ashamed that they didn't know where to hide their faces.

'We shall pass judgement again. Catch the fellow right now!' ordered the king.

But there was no one to obey him! All his men were now kings and they had no desire to carry out his orders!

The minister alone went forward to catch Dukhiram.

Dukhiram said, 'What will you do if I have to be hanged? Who will do it? The hangman is now a king! The king and you will have to become hangmen.'

As soon as he said that, the king and the minister were transformed into two dark, ugly executioners waiting for orders with axes in their hands! Now who would give them orders?

Dukhiram had gradually come to realize that whatever wish he expressed would come true. For a moment, he thought of all the things he could do with his powers.

But Dukhiram was a good man. He suppressed the thought and merely said, 'Your Highness, I was your servant. I am still grateful to you. Your kingdom will remain yours. Kindly allow me to leave.'

The king stood with his head bowed in shame. He too had realized what enormous powers Dukhiram had. What could he say in reply? He only said, 'You could have taken away my kingdom. You could have killed me if you had wanted to. I have understood at last that you are a great man. Half my kingdom is yours. Marry my daughter and live in peace!'

So Dukhiram got married to the princess and ruled his kingdom wisely and they lived happily ever after.

And what happened to the rest of them? Dukhiram hadn't said anything about the minister. So he remained a hangman.

All the men who had become kings faced a new problem. They were kings, but they didn't have kingdoms to rule! They all said, 'I am a king now. Why should I work?' Things became very difficult.

Finally, Dukhiram said, 'There's no need for all of you to be kings. Go back and do what you are good at. And live in peace.'

THE MONKEY PRINCE

This is the story of a king who had seven queens, but no children. This made the king very sad. He sat grumpily in his court and replied rudely when anyone spoke to him.

One day a sage came to see the king. When he saw the glum look on the king's face, he asked, 'Why are you so sad?'

'I have everything one can wish for,' replied the king. 'I have a large kingdom, plenty of money, many servants. But I don't have a child. Who will look after everything when I die?'

'Is that all?' said the sage. 'There's no need for you to worry. When you wake up tomorrow, go straight towards the north. After walking for some distance, you will reach a forest. At the edge of the forest, you will see a mango tree. Pluck seven mangoes from the forest and give them to your seven queens. After eating the mangoes the queens will give birth to seven sons. But a word of caution—don't look back when you are bringing the mangoes!'

The sage went away. The rest of the day and the night passed very slowly for the king.

When dawn came, the king got out of bed and started walking north. After walking a long way, he reached the edge of the forest. Sure enough, he found a mango tree there. He could also see seven mangoes on the tree. Though the king had come to the forest several times on hunting trips, he had never seen the mango tree before. He quickly climbed the tree, plucked the mangoes and started walking back home.

He had barely taken a few steps when a voice called out from behind him:

Cast your eyes on what's behind—
Take more mangoes of a better kind.

In his excitement at the sage's words coming true, the king had forgotten all about his warning and he turned around.

As soon as he looked back, all the mangoes escaped from his hands, flew back up the tree and hung from its branches as though they had never been plucked! The king remembered the warning now, but it was too late!

The king had to go back and pluck the mangoes all over again. This time he was determined not to look back. As he started back, several voices called out to him. Some cursed him. One of them called him a thief. The king paid no attention and walked quickly towards the palace.

When he reached home, he gave the seven mangoes to the six older queens. The youngest queen was not there at that time. 'Take these mangoes. Make them into a paste and share them among the seven of you,' he told them.

The six queens followed his instructions, but they did not save a share for the youngest queen. But the youngest queen's maid saw what had happened.

After the other queens had finished eating, the maid took the skins of all the mangoes, which the six queens peeled off before they made the paste. She ground them to a fine paste and took the paste to the youngest queen. 'Have this medicine, my dear. It will do you good,' she said. The queen believed her and had the 'medicine'.

Very soon, the six queens who had eaten the mangoes gave birth to six beautiful sons. The king was overjoyed. He celebrated the birth of the princes in a grand way. There was music and dancing, and the people rejoiced.

Soon after, the youngest queen also gave birth, but to a baby monkey! Seeing the monkey, the king was enraged and threw the queen out of the palace.

The people of the kingdom felt sad for the queen, who was kind and gentle. They built a small hut for her.' Stay here, beloved queen,' they said to her.

The queen started living in the hut with her child.

The monkey prince grew up quickly. He learnt to speak at a very young age. He was very bright and soon knew a lot about human manners and behaviour. But he also spent a lot of his time swinging from trees and fed on fruits. If he liked a fruit very much, he brought it home for his mother. People did not mind when he climbed their trees and plucked their fruits. They all loved him and wondered at his intelligence.

The years went by. The six princes also grew up. They hated the monkey prince. They would throw stones at him and chase him away if he came to play with them.

One day the monkey prince saw his brothers with their tutor. The princes were reading their books, while the tutor was explaining things to them.

The monkey prince went to his mother and said, 'Get me some books. I want to read too.'

His mother wept when she heard this. 'How will you read?' she asked. 'You are a monkey!'

'I promise you I'll be able to read,' said her son, 'if you get me some books and teach me.'

The monkey prince started reading. He was so bright that it took him only two days to finish any book his mother brought for him. Within two years, he had read most of the books she could find in the city, and became very learned. By that time his brothers had reluctantly managed to finish reading two or three books and were constantly being scolded by their tutor.

When the king heard about the monkey prince and his mastery of books, he was furious. 'What! A monkey with brains!' he said. 'Bring him here! I want to see him!'

The monkey prince was never scared of anything. When he heard that the king wanted to see him, he went to meet him immediately.

When the king spoke to him, he liked the monkey prince tremendously. The king had also started feeling guilty that he had thrown the youngest queen out of his palace. He couldn't bring her back because his other queens wouldn't like it. So he built a beautiful house for her next to the palace. She started living there with her son. When she needed money, the king's men would bring it for her. People called her house 'the monkey's house'. The other princes were now jealous of the monkey prince and hated him even more.

When the princes grew up, people said it was time they got married. 'Let them travel all over the world,' said the king. 'They will see new places, learn a lot and bring home six beautiful young brides.' Everyone agreed that this was a good plan.

So the princes dressed up in fine clothes, took plenty of money and set off on their horses to explore new lands. Seeing them leave, the monkey prince said to his mother, 'I want to go too.'

'What will you do with them?' asked his mother. 'No princess will want to marry you. Besides, how will I live here without you?'

'I'll return in no time at all,' said the monkey prince. 'Please, dear mother, let me go!'

The queen had no choice but to let her son go.

The six princes left the palace far behind and rode through a forest. From behind the trees appeared the monkey prince. 'My brothers, I want to go too,' he said. 'Take me along with you.'

The princes were furious. 'How dare you call us your brothers!' they cried. 'You want to come with us and marry a princess! Just wait and see what we do to you!'

They beat up the poor monkey till he was black and blue, tied him to a tree and rode on happily.

A band of bandits lived in that forest. They saw six princes dressed in splendid robes riding past them. Swiftly, they surrounded the princes from all sides. The princes were so frightened that they forgot to take out their swords! Within minutes, the bandits robbed them of their money and their clothes. They tied the princes up firmly, lashed them on to their horses and led the horses along.

The bandits took the princes back to their lair. On the way, they saw the monkey tied to a tree. They took him along as well. But they thought the monkey was someone's pet, abandoned in the jungle, so did not bother to tie him too firmly, but just put a noose around his neck so that he followed them.

The monkey was so pleased to be freed from the tree that he skipped and danced on the way.

The bandits' lair was deep inside the forest. They had been riding since morning, and were very tired by the time they reached home. So they left the bound princes and the monkey in one room, had dinner and went to sleep. Soon loud snores could be heard through the locked door.

The monkey prince quickly untied himself and then set the princes free. The princes were so grateful to him that they couldn't leave him behind. So they took all their things and rode away as fast as they could with the monkey prince. The robbers slept on.

The princes rode through the night without stopping. In the morning, they reached a beautiful city, which was the capital of another kingdom. They could see the king's palace in the distance. It looked like a white, luminous mountain.

The six princes rode up to the palace and walked boldly in. Seeing their fine clothes and their princely manner, the guards let them in without stopping them. But the monkey knew that he wouldn't be allowed to enter the palace. So he went to the back of the palace, where there was a pond and lay down beside it.

The king of this land also had seven queens. The first six were ugly and jealous of the youngest queen, who was beautiful and kind. The six queens had poisoned the king's mind against her and had driven her out of the palace. She now lived in a small hut behind the palace, by the pond near which the monkey prince was resting.

The six queens had six daughters, who were as ugly as their mothers and just as mean. The youngest queen also had a daughter—a lovely and gracious girl. But the six wicked queens had told the king all kinds of lies about the youngest princess when she was born. They said that she was ugly, hunchbacked, deaf, dumb, lame and mad! The king believed their lies and had never set eyes on his youngest daughter.

When the monkey prince had been by the pond for a while, the six princesses came there to bathe. The youngest princess also joined them. As they were bathing, the youngest princess accidentally splashed some water on the monkey. The other princesses started teasing their youngest sister. 'This monkey is now your husband,' they said.

When the six evil queens heard what had happened, they also cried, 'The youngest princess has married a monkey!'

Soon everyone in the court, including the king, believed that the princess had indeed married a monkey.

When the youngest queen heard of this, she was too sad for words. She clutched the princess to her bosom, and cried and cried.

The monkey prince heard her weep. He came and stood at the door of the hut. 'Don't cry, dear queen,' he said very gently. 'Everything will be all right.'

When the queen heard the monkey speak, she stopped crying. All her sorrows magically disappeared. She was very pleased to hear that the monkey was a prince, and she found herself believing him when he said that all would be well.

The monkey started living on top of a tree next to the hut. He looked after the queen and the princess as best as he could. The queen soon forgot that he was a monkey, as he was kinder and more intelligent than any person she knew.

Meanwhile, there was much excitement at the court about the other six princes. When they had arrived at the court, everyone could make out from their appearance and behaviour that they were indeed princes.

'Who are you and what do you want?' the king asked them after they had been made welcome. When he heard their father's name and learnt that they had come there looking for brides, his joy knew no bounds.

'Your father is my friend,' he said to the princes. 'I will be delighted to get you married to my six daughters.'

Just then the princes heard someone in the court say that the youngest princess had wed a monkey. The princes understood at once that the monkey they were talking about was their own brother. You can't imagine how jealous they were to hear that! The monkey had married a princess before they had! They also heard people whisper that the youngest princess was the loveliest and the most sweet-natured. The more they thought about it, the angrier they felt.

Anyway, the six princes were soon married to the six princesses. Then the king sent them off in a beautiful boat shaped like a peacock. The monkey prince and his wife said goodbye to the youngest queen and followed them in a small boat.

The six princes were determined not to let the monkey return home with his princess. But they didn't let the monkey guess that they were envious. In fact, they were more friendly and affectionate than usual all through the journey.

The night before they reached their own country, the six princes climbed into the monkey prince's boat. He was asleep. They tied his hands and feet and threw him into the water.

Fortunately, the youngest princess had woken up from the noise they made. She quickly flung a pillow at the monkey prince and he managed to stay afloat and reach the river bank.

The princes reached the palace the next morning. Their father, the king, heard of their arrival and went to receive them and their brides himself. The six princes touched his feet to show him their respect and loyalty.

After the king had welcomed them and the six princesses, he asked, 'Where is my monkey?'

'Alas! The monkey got drowned in the river,' the princes said, trying to look sad.

But the monkey hadn't drowned. He had reached the bank before the other princes had. He was hiding behind a tree and watching them. When he heard his brothers say he had drowned, he came forward and touched the king's feet. 'I haven't died, father,' he said. 'My brothers tied me up and threw me into the river. I've managed to reach here with great difficulty.'

The princes were horrified to see that he was alive, and even more upset when he spoke.

'Is this what you have done?' shouted the enraged king. 'Leave my kingdom at once! I don't want to see you again!'

After he had got rid of his wicked sons, the king brought the monkey prince and his mother to his palace. You can imagine how happy the queen was to have her son back. Now she also had a wonderful daughter-in-law.

Soon the monkey prince's wife discovered that her husband was a monkey only during the day. At night he would take off his monkey-skin and change into a handsome prince. The princess reported her discovery to the queen, who then told the king.

The king said to his daughter-in-law, 'Burn the monkey-skin when he takes it off.'

That night, a huge fire was lit next to the monkey prince's bedchamber. When he took off his skin and went to sleep, the princess tiptoed in, took his skin and burnt it.

When the monkey prince got up in the morning, he searched high and low but could not find his skin. He felt very embarrassed, for now everyone would know his secret. But there was nothing he could do about it. He couldn't change into a monkey any more.

Soon everyone in the country got to know the truth. People came from all over the kingdom to see their prince and went back dancing with joy!

THE GHANGOSAUR'S TALE

Once upon a time there was a king who had a lovely daughter. But from the day she was born, the princess was always ill. She was never well—not even for a single day.

The king summoned many doctors from all over the world, who examined her, scratched their heads, looked wise and gave her all kinds of medicines. But none of the medicines were any good. Instead of getting better, the princess grew thinner and weaker every year.

The king had all the wealth anyone could wish for, but he was always very sad. He constantly worried about his daughter.

Years went by. One day a holy man came to visit the king. When he heard about the princess's illness, he said, 'Your Highness, if your daughter has the juice of one lemon, she will get well.'

The holy man said that and went away. One lemon! The king had only a vague idea what a lemon was, and absolutely no idea where he could get one from. So he called all his subjects and made a solemn announcement: 'My daughter needs the juice of a lemon to get better. Whoever brings me that lemon will get the princess as his bride. I will also give him my kingdom.'

The trouble was that lemon trees were not common in that land! There was only *one* lemon tree in *one* farmer's garden in the whole kingdom! The farmer had brought the tree from Sylhet. The tree had just started bearing fruit that year. And the lemons of that tree were no ordinary lemons. Each of them was as big as a pumpkin! None of you have ever seen or tasted lemons like those. I haven't either.

The farmer had three sons: Jodu, Goshto and Manik. When the farmer heard the king's announcement, he gave Jodu a basket of lemons. 'Take these quickly to the king's house,' he said. 'If the princess has a lemon and gets better, you will get to marry her and rule the kingdom.'

So Jodu took the basket and started walking towards the king's palace. On the way, he met a man who was only one foot tall.

'What do you have in your basket?' asked the man.

'Frogs,' replied Jodu.

The man said, 'So be it,' and went his way.

Jodu reached the palace. When the guards heard that he was carrying lemons, they treated him with great respect and took him to the king.

The king was very pleased. He eagerly opened the basket. As soon as he did that, four frogs leaped out of the basket and climbed on to the king's turban! All the lemons in the basket had turned into frogs!

Jodu did not get to marry the princess. In fact, he was lucky he reached home alive.

The following day, the farmer gave Goshto a basket of lemons so that he could try his luck.

On his way to the palace, Goshto too met the man who was only one foot tall.

'What do you have in your basket?' asked the man.

'Pumpkin seeds,' replied Goshto.

And the one-foot-tall man said, 'So be it.'

This time the guards refused to let Goshto enter through the gates. It was only after much begging and pleading that they let him in. You can imagine what happened after that.

Manik was the simplest of the three brothers. So no one asked Manik to take lemons to the king. If his two brothers had failed, there was no way Manik was going to succeed.

But Manik was determined to go. He pleaded so much with his father that he had to agree in the end. Manik set off for the palace with a third basket of lemons.

On the way, Manik met the strange, short man. 'What do you have in your basket?' asked the man.

'There are lemons in the basket,' replied Manik. 'They will help the princess get well.'

'So be it,' said the short man, and went away smiling.

It wasn't easy for Manik to enter the king's palace. He had to beg and plead for hours. When the guards finally allowed him in, they warned him, 'If there are frogs or pumpkin seeds in your basket, you won't come out alive.'

But when the basket was opened, there were only lemons in the basket. The king was very pleased. He quickly sent the lemons to the princess. 'I am waiting here,' he told his servant. 'Come and tell me what happens.'

While they were waiting, the princess herself came with the news. The lemons had cured her miraculously!

The king was overjoyed. But only for a moment. The next moment he started thinking, 'What have I done? Now I'll have to let my daughter marry a farmer's son!' He decided promptly that he would not keep his word to Manik.

'Now the princess will be mine,' Manik thought to himself and smiled happily, for the princess was indeed beautiful.

The king interrupted his daydreaming. 'You have done well,' he said. 'But marrying a princess is not all that easy. You will have to perform one more task for me. You must build me a boat that runs as fast on land as it does on water. Unless you bring me this boat, I am afraid you do not get to marry the princess!'

Manik went back home sadly, and told his brothers what had happened. Jodu and Goshto considered their youngest brother a fool. They thought that if Manik could cure the princess, anyone could build the boat the king desired.

Jodu took an axe and set off immediately. He went into the forest, cut some wood and started making the boat.

He worked hard because he wanted to finish his work the same day.

Suddenly the strange, short man appeared from nowhere. 'What are you making?' he asked.

'A tub,' replied Jodu.

'So be it,' said the man and went away.

Jodu continued with his work, but all his efforts were useless. The wood refused to be made into a boat. Whatever he did, the wood took the shape of a tub. Enraged, Jodu flung away the tub, took another piece of wood and started working all over again. But it was of no use. However hard he tried to make a boat, he always ended up with a tub.

In the end, Jodu gave up and returned home carrying three tubs! The tubs were too good to be left in the forest.

Next, it was Goshto's turn to try to build the boat. The strange, short man appeared again and Goshto came back carrying five ploughs!

When Manik went to build the boat on the third day, and the strange, short man asked him what he was making, Manik told him the truth. 'I am building a boat that will run as fast on land as it will on water,' he said. 'If I build such a boat, the king will let me marry his daughter.'

'So be it,' said the strange, short man.

Manik had just cut some wood and was sitting on it. As soon as the strange, short man uttered the magic words, Manik found he was sitting in a splendid boat. There were no oars or sails or boatman, but it started racing through the forest. When the boat reached water, it floated equally swiftly. It seemed to know exactly where it was supposed to go.

Manik looked around the boat in delight. Not only was it swift, it was also beautiful. It was lined with velvet cushions, fit for a king. The outside was beautifully decorated with things found only in the land of the one-foot-tall man.

The king was seated in his court when, all of a sudden, the boat arrived carrying Manik. Everyone in the court was astonished by the beauty of the boat, and by the fact that it could travel on land.

The king was also amazed, but he didn't show it. His mind was working furiously. 'This is not enough,' he said to Manik. 'You will have to do something more for me. You will have to fetch me a feather from the tail of the Ghangosaur. It will add to the beauty of my crown. When you get me the feather, you can marry my daughter.'

The Ghangosaur was a terrible creature—one-third bird, one-third beast and one-third demon. He had a hideous face and a nasty temper, and he was very learned and extremely rich. He lived in a golden palace on the bank of an unnamed river in a land far, far away, about a month's journey away from Manik's homeland. Whenever he saw a human being, he just caught hold of him and gobbled him up! No man had ever talked to him and lived to tell the tale.

Manik set off to fetch a feather from the tail of this awful creature. On the way, he asked the people he met for directions to the land of the Ghangosaur. They told him, trembling with fear. And Manik went straight ahead, without looking to his right or left. At night, he would take shelter in the nearest house. When people heard that Manik was going to meet the Ghangosaur, they were all very kind and hospitable to him. In the morning, he would start off again.

One night Manik stayed at a rich man's house. After they had talked a while, the rich man said, 'You are going to meet the Ghangosaur. He knows about a lot of things. I have lost the keys of my treasure chest. Please ask the Ghangosaur where the keys could be.'

'I will,' replied Manik.

Another night he stayed at another wealthy man's house. His daughter was very ill. No doctor had been able to diagnose what was wrong with her. 'Please find out from the Ghangosaur how to cure my daughter,' the man told Manik.

'I will,' promised Manik.

After travelling for a whole month, Manik finally reached the banks of the unnamed river. He could see the golden palace of the Ghangosaur on the other side. There were no bridges or boats to take him across. But there was an old man who carried people across the river on his back. Manik clambered on to his back to be taken across.

On the way, the old man said, 'Please ask the Ghangosaur when my troubles will be over. I can't eat. I can't sleep. I carry people across the river all day, all night. I have been doing this since my childhood. Now I am an old man. Maybe the Ghangosaur can help me.'

'I will ask him,' said Manik as the old man set him down on the opposite bank.

When Manik reached the palace of the terrible Ghangosaur, he wasn't home, but his wife was. As soon as she saw Manik, she turned pale and said, 'Run away, boy! Run away as fast as you can! The Ghangosaur will gobble you up the moment he sees you!'

'But I have come here to take a feather from his tail. How can I go back without taking it? And I want to know where to find the lost keys of the treasure chest and how to cure the rich man's daughter. The man who carried me across the river wants to know how his troubles will end. I have to meet the Ghangosaur and ask him all these questions.'

'Who are you?' asked the Ghangosaur's wife. 'Instead of running for your life, you want to pluck feathers from the tail of the Ghangosaur! And you want to ask him a hundred questions!'

'I am Manik,' he replied. 'The king won't let me marry his daughter unless I get the feathers. That is why I am here.'

The Ghangosaur's wife was a kind-hearted creature. She felt sorry for Manik. 'All right. You hide under the bed,' she said. 'If you are lucky, you will get what you want.'

Late in the evening, the Ghangosaur returned home. His wife had laid out his dinner on a golden plate on his table. But the Ghangosaur was a very suspicious creature. He could always tell when something was wrong. He took a few deep breaths and said, 'I can smell a human being!

Aah! A human being! Bring him here! I will have him for dinner tonight!'

When Manik heard the Ghangosaur's words, his heart skipped a beat. The Ghangosaur's wife was also very nervous. But she quickly made up a story. She told the Ghangosaur that a man had come to their house, but had run away after she told him about the Ghangosaur. The Ghangosaur believed her and sat down to eat.

After dinner, the Ghangosaur lay down on his bed and promptly fell asleep. His tail did not fit inside the quilt, and dangled down the side of the bed.

Manik saw his opportunity. He reached out an arm and plucked a feather from the tail.

The Ghangosaur woke up with a start. 'Who pulled my tail?' he asked. 'Hmm…I can smell a human being again!'

'You are mistaken,' said his wife. 'Your tail is so large that it must have got stuck somewhere. A man had come here, as I told you. He told me many stories. He told me about a rich man who had lost the keys of his treasure chest…'

Before she could finish her story, the Ghangosaur said 'Oh yes! The keys of the treasure chest! I know where they are! The man's youngest son has hidden them in a hole in a mattress!'

'The man told me about a girl who is ill…' continued the wife.

The Ghangosaur grunted and said, 'A frog has taken a hair belonging to this girl and hidden it in a hole in the ground. If someone can find the hole and take out the hair, the girl will get better.'

His wife said, 'An old man helps people cross the river by carrying people on his back...'

'He is very stupid,' said the Ghangosaur. 'He carries so many people across the river. He should just put one of them down in the middle of the river! Then he will be free to go home. The other man will have to continue his work.'

Manik's problems were now all solved. He waited until morning. The Ghangosaur had breakfast and left for work. His wife gave Manik some food for the journey and bade him farewell.

On his way back home, the first person he met was the old man. 'Did you speak to the Ghangosaur about me?' he asked Manik.

'I'll tell you. But you must take me across the river first. I am in a hurry,' said Manik.

After he reached the other bank, Manik told the old man, 'You must put someone down in the middle of the river. Then you can go home.'

'I am so grateful to you, I feel like carrying you across the river two more times!' said the old man.

'What you have done for me is enough,' said Manik. 'I don't want to trouble you any more. Now I must return home.'

After walking for four days, Manik reached the house of the rich man whose daughter was ill. He stayed with him again.

'Did the Ghangosaur say anything about my daughter?' asked his host very eagerly.

'Yes,' replied Manik.

The hole in the ground was found and the hair was taken out. The girl had been lying in bed for the last two years. She got up and started walking about the house, completely cured! Everyone in the family was overjoyed. They gave so much money to Manik that he needed ten camels to carry it all home.

There was similar rejoicing at the house of the man who had lost his keys. He, too, rewarded Manik generously.

Manik took all the money, returned home and presented the feathers to the king. People praised Manik to the skies. They all felt that the king had tested Manik enough and that the wedding should take place immediately. The king had no way out this time. Reluctantly, he agreed to let the two of them get married.

The wedding took place with great pomp and pageantry. Manik had brought so much money that he and the princess could live comfortably all their lives.

The king was the only person who was not happy. 'If there is so much money in the land of the Ghangosaur, I must go there and get some for myself,' he thought to himself.

After the wedding, the king set off to go to the land of the Ghangosaur. But he never managed to reach his palace. That is because the old man put him down in the middle of the river!

At first, the king was surprised; then he was angry. After that, he started calling the old man names. Soon he was begging him to come back.

But the old man had no time to listen to him. He crossed the river and ran as fast as his legs could carry him. In his hurry, he forgot to tell the king how the king could also escape. That is why the king is there even today carrying people on his back!

If any of you visit the land of the Ghangosaur, please tell the king the secret he doesn't know. But a word of caution: Tell him the secret *after* he has brought you back to this side of the river. Otherwise, things may turn out to be a little difficult.

TALES OF GRANDMOTHERS

CLEVER GRANNY HUNCHBACK

Once upon a time there lived an old woman with a hunchback. Everyone called her Granny Hunchback. She walked with a stick, and when she walked, her head bobbed from side to side. She had two dogs: one was called Ranga and the other was called Bhanga.

One day Granny Hunchback decided to visit her granddaughter. She told her dogs, 'You two stay at home.'

'All right,' said Ranga and Bhanga.

Granny Hunchback started off. She walked with her stick and her head bobbed from side to side.

A fox saw her and said, 'Oho, there's that Granny Hunchback. Granny, I want to eat you!'

'Wait, let me go to my granddaughter's house,' replied Granny Hunchback. 'I'll come back nice and plump. Eat me then. Right now, I am just skin and bones, so what is the point of eating me?'

'All right,' said the fox. 'Come back nice and plump, then I will eat you.' And he went away.

Granny set off again. She walked with her stick and her head bobbed from side to side.

After she had walked some more, a tiger saw her and said, 'Oho, there's that Granny Hunchback. Granny, I want to eat you!'

'Wait, let me go to my granddaughter's house,' replied Granny Hunchback. 'I'll come back nice and plump. Eat me then. Right now, I am just skin and bones, what is the point of eating me?'

'All right,' said the tiger. 'Come back nice and plump, then I will eat you.' And the tiger, too, went away.

Granny set off once more. She walked with her stick and her head bobbed from side to side.

After she had gone a bit further, a bear saw her and said, 'Oho, there's that Granny Hunchback. Granny, I want to eat you!'

'Wait, let me go to my granddaughter's house,' replied Granny Hunchback. 'I'll come back nice and plump. Eat me then. Right now, I am just skin and bones, what is the point of eating me?'

'All right,' said the bear. 'Come back nice and plump, then I will eat you.'

The bear, too, went away.

Granny Hunchback reached her granddaughter's house. There she gorged on sweets and became so fat that if she ate just a bit more she would have surely burst!

So she called her granddaughter and said, 'I have to go home, but I can't even walk! I'll have to roll all the way home! And the bear, the tiger and the fox are eagerly waiting for me. They'll catch me and eat me up. Now what do I do?'

'Don't worry, Granny,' said her granddaughter. 'I'll put you inside this pumpkin shell. The bear, the tiger and the fox won't know that it's you and they won't be able to eat you.'

She put Granny inside a big round pumpkin shell, and gave her tamarind and rice to eat. Then she gave the shell a big heave, and it began rolling.

The pumpkin rolled, and Granny, sitting inside, sang:

Roll pumpkin, roll pumpkin,
Roll, my mighty car.
Eating rice and tamarind
Granny travels far!

The bear was waiting by the road to catch and eat Granny Hunchback. But instead of Granny wobbling towards him, he saw a pumpkin rolling along.

He examined the pumpkin carefully. Neither was it Granny, nor was it anything he could eat. And someone inside was singing: 'Granny travels far.' So the bear thought that Granny had given him the slip. In his disappointment, he angrily gave the pumpkin a big push and went home hungry.

The pumpkin rolled faster, and Granny, sitting inside, sang:

Roll pumpkin, roll pumpkin,
Roll, my mighty car.
Eating rice and tamarind
Granny travels far!

Some distance down the road, the tiger was waiting to eat Granny. But instead of Granny wobbling towards him, he saw a pumpkin rolling along.

He examined the pumpkin carefully. Neither was it Granny, nor was it anything he could eat. And someone inside was singing: 'Granny travels far.' So the tiger thought that Granny had given him the slip. In his disappointment, he angrily gave the pumpkin a big push and went home hungry.

The pumpkin kept rolling, and Granny, sitting inside, sang:

Roll pumpkin, roll pumpkin,
Roll, my mighty car.
Eating rice and tamarind
Granny travels far!

A bit further on, there sat the fox. He saw the pumpkin and sneered, 'A talking pumpkin! I have to see what's inside!' He kicked open the pumpkin shell and saw Granny inside. 'Oho,' he said, 'I'll eat you now!'

'Certainly,' said Granny Hunchback. 'Why else would I have come? But don't you want to hear a song first?'

'That's not a bad idea,' admitted the fox. 'In fact, I am not a bad singer either.'

'Oh, that's very good,' said Granny. 'Let us then sit on this rock and sing.'

She sat on the rock and sang very loudly: 'Ranga, Bhanga, come quickly, come quickly-y-y-y-y-y!'

Her dogs came running at once. One caught the fox by the neck, the other by his back, and they pulled very hard.

That was the end of the fox.

And that is the tale of how clever Granny Hunchback came back safely from her granddaughter's house.

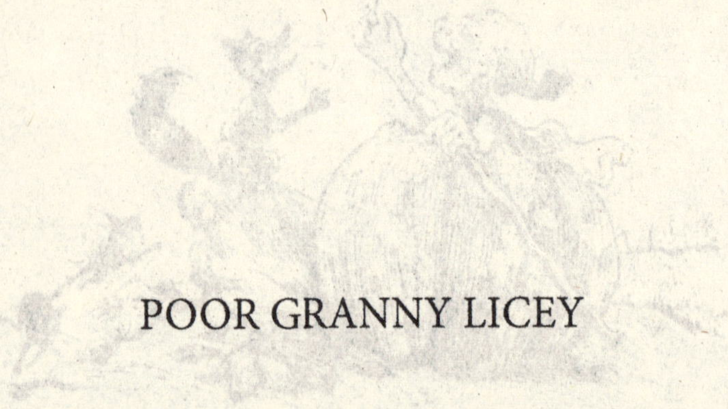

POOR GRANNY LICEY

Once upon a time there was an old woman whose hair was crawling with lice. So everyone called her Granny Licey. Wherever she went, lice would keep falling from her head. Even when she served her husband his meals, lice would drop on to his plate.

One day the old man got so angry that he gave her one hard blow with his stick. At that, Granny Licey threw her pot of rice down so that it smashed to pieces and went off down the bank of the river. The old man tried to call her back, but she would not listen to him.

There was a stork standing by the river. 'Where are you going, Granny Licey?' he asked.

'My old man beat me, and I'm never going to go back home again,' she replied.

'But why did he beat you?' asked the stork.

'Because lice from my hair fell on his plate,' said Granny Licey.

'But lice taste so good!' said the stork. 'Why did he beat you for that? He must be mad. Why don't you come and stay in my house? I've heard that you cook very well and I have no one to cook for me.'

So Granny Licey went to live with the stork and cooked for him. The stork liked her cooking, and if lice fell into his plate, he really loved it.

One day the stork brought a big fish home. 'Cook it well, Granny Licey,' he told her and went off to the river bank.

Granny Licey began cooking, but she suddenly felt dizzy and fell into the pot head first.

When the stork came home, he found poor Granny lying quite dead in the pot. He was so unhappy that he went back to the river bank and cried for seven days, not even bothering to stop to eat anything.

'He has been here for seven days and he hasn't eaten a bite! Whatever could have happened to him?' wondered the river. He decided to ask him. 'Stork, my friend, what's wrong?' he said.

'Whatever had to happen has happened,' said the stork. 'There's no point talking about it.'

'No, you *must* tell me about it,' insisted the river.

'If I tell you, all your water will froth and turn white,' said the stork.

'Let it froth and turn white,' replied the river. 'Tell me your story.'

So the stork said:

Poor old Granny Licey died,
For seven days the stork cried.

As soon as he said this, all the water in the river foamed and turned white.

An elephant used to come to the river every day to drink. That day, he came and was amazed to find the river frothing over. 'What's happened to you?' he asked. 'How did all your water froth and turn white?'

'If I tell you how, your tail will fall off and disappear,' replied the river.

'Let it fall off and disappear,' said the elephant. 'Tell me your story.'

So the river said:

Poor old Granny Licey died,
For seven days the stork cried,
All my waters turned to white!

As soon as he said this, the elephant's tail fell off with a thump in the bushes, and he could not find it any more.

Some time later, the elephant was walking by a tree. 'Oh! Whatever happened to you?' asked the surprised tree. 'Where did your tail go?'

'If I tell you, all your leaves will fall off,' said the elephant.

'Let them all fall off,' said the tree. 'Tell me your story.'

So the elephant said:

Poor old Granny Licey died,
For seven days the stork cried,
All the waters turned to white,
And my tail fell out of sight!

As soon as he said this, all the leaves on the tree fell off.

A bird had her nest in the tree. She had gone looking for food. When she came back, she found the tree totally bare. 'Tree, what happened?' she exclaimed. 'Where have all your leaves gone?'

'If I tell you, you will lose one eye,' said the tree.

'That doesn't matter,' said the bird. 'Tell me your story.'

So the tree said:

Poor old Granny Licey died,
For seven days the stork cried,
All the waters turned to white,
Elephant's tail fell out of sight,
And I all my leaves did shed!

As soon as the tree said this, the bird found she could see only through one eye.

The bird went looking for food in a field, where the king's cowherd saw her. 'What's happened to your eye?' asked the cowherd.

'If I tell you, your stick will get stuck to your hand,' warned the bird.

'Let it get stuck,' said the cowherd. 'Tell me your story.'

So the bird said:

Poor old Granny Licey died,
For seven days the stork cried,
All the waters turned to white,
Elephant's tail fell out of sight,
The tree all her leaves did shed,
And I lost one eye from my head!

As soon as she said this, the cowherd's stick got stuck to his hand. He tried very hard to shake it off, but the stick stayed stuck. When he went back to the king's palace with the cows, he was still shaking his hand, trying to get the stick off.

The queen's maid was sifting rice with a sieve. 'Why are you shaking your hand like a fool?' she asked angrily, adjusting her headband. 'What's happened to your hand?'

'If I tell you, your sieve will get stuck to your headband,' said the cowherd.

'Let it get stuck,' said the maid. 'Tell me your story.'

So the cowherd said:

Poor old Granny Licey died,
For seven days the stork cried,
All the waters turned to white,

Elephant's tail fell out of sight,
The tree all her leaves did shed,
The bird lost one eye from her head,
And my stick stuck to my hand!

As soon as he said this, the maid's sieve got stuck to her headband. She shook her head up and down, but it stayed stuck. She pulled at it with both hands, but she could not budge it. She banged her head on the ground, but to no effect. She sat down on the floor and howled and howled, but she could not get rid of the sieve. Finally, she gave up and went to the queen's kitchen.

The queen was about to serve the king his lunch. As she was taking his golden dish to the dining hall, she noticed the maid and asked, 'What's happened? Why do you have a sieve stuck to your head?'

'If I tell you, Your Highness, the king's golden dish will get stuck to your hand,' said the maid.

'Tell me your story,' said the queen, 'and let us see how that dish gets stuck.'

So the maid said:

Poor old Granny Licey died,
For seven days the stork cried,
All the waters turned to white,
Elephant's tail fell out of sight,
The tree all her leaves did shed,

The bird lost one eye from her head,
The cowherd's stick stuck to his hand,
And the sieve stuck to my headband!

As soon as she finished, the king's golden dish got stuck to the queen's hand. She couldn't get rid of it. What could she do now? She served rice on another golden dish and took it to the king.

'Why are you holding that other dish?' asked the king.

'If I tell you, Sire, you will not be able to get up,' said the queen. 'You will get stuck to your chair.'

This made the king laugh very hard. He said, 'Tell me your story anyway.'

So the queen said:

Poor old Granny Licey died,
For seven days the stork cried,
All the waters turned to white,
Elephant's tail fell out of sight,
The tree all her leaves did shed,
The bird lost one eye from her head,
The cowherd's stick stuck to his hand,
The maid's sieve stuck to her headband,
The dish stuck to my hand so fair!

As soon as she said this, the king got stuck to his chair. He pulled and pushed and heaved but he could not get up from the chair. All the king's men tried very hard too, but even they could not get the king up. Finally, four of them carried the king to the court in his chair.

When the people in the court saw the king, they did not know what to do. They thought it was very funny, but they dared not laugh, because that would make the king angry. And they were too scared to ask the king what had happened.

Then the king himself asked, 'You must all want to know how I got stuck in my chair?'

'Yes, Your Majesty,' they said respectfully.

'If I tell you, all of you will also get stuck to your seats,' warned the king.

'If our king can get stuck, so can we!' they all cried.

So the king said:

Poor old Granny Licey died,
For seven days the stork cried,
All the waters turned to white,
Elephant's tail fell out of sight,
The tree all her leaves did shed,
The bird lost one eye from her head,
The cowherd's stick stuck to his hand,
The maid's sieve stuck to her headband,
The dish stuck to queen's hand so fair,
And I got stuck to this chair!

As soon as they heard this, all the king's men no longer felt like laughing. They had all got stuck to their seats.

Luckily for them all, there was a very wise barber in that land. 'Call a carpenter quickly,' said he.

The carpenter came and cut the chair off the king's bottom, and the seats off the king's men. A little wood still remained stuck on everyone's backside. This had to be scraped off later.

The dish was cut from the queen's hand, and the sieve was cut from the maid's headband, and the stick was cut from the cowherd's hand and thrown away. And they all heaved a big sigh of relief.

But the poor elephant never got his tail back, nor the bird her eye.

TALES OF BIRDS

HOW TUNTUNI FOOLED THE PUSSYCAT

Behind the farmer's house were many brinjal bushes, which grew thick and big.

It was such a big bush that Tuntuni, the little tailor bird, had sewn together some leaves with her beak and made a cosy nest for herself.

Inside the nest were her three chicks. They were very small. They could not fly. They could not even open their eyes. All they could do was open their mouths and say: 'Chi chi...'

The farmer's pussycat was very wicked. She dreamed all the time of eating Tuntuni's chicks, especially as the nest was not very high up.

One day, she came to the brinjal bush and called out, 'Dear Tuntuni, how are you?'

Tuntuni bowed her head low to touch the branch she was sitting on and curtsied and said, 'Hail to the Queen!'

Pussycat went off, very pleased with herself.

Then Pussycat began coming every day. Every day, Tuntuni would bow and curtsey, and Pussycat would go back happy.

Soon Tuntuni's chicks grew up. They now had beautiful small wings. They could also now keep their eyes open.

Tuntuni asked them, 'Will you be able to fly, my darlings?'

And they said, 'Yes, Mama.'

Tuntuni asked, 'Will you be able to fly to the top of that very tall palm tree?'

So the chicks flew and sat on the top of the very tall palm tree. Tuntuni was very happy. 'Just you wait, you wicked pussycat,' she thought.

A little while later, Pussycat came and asked, 'What are you doing, dear Tuntuni?'

Tuntuni lifted her leg, aimed a kick at her and said, 'Get lost, you evil pussycat!' And away she flew.

Pussycat snarled and jumped up on the bush. But she could neither catch Tuntuni nor eat her little chicks. All she got were pricks all over her body from the thorns, and she had to go back home limping and angry.

HOW TUNTUNI SCARED THE BARBER

Dancing on the leaves of the brinjal bush, Tuntuni the little tailor bird got a thorn in her foot. Her foot swelled up till there was a big boil.

What could she do now? How could she cure such a big boil?

She went around asking people. Everyone told her, 'Get a barber to lance it.'

So Tuntuni went to the barber. 'Mr Barber, Mr Barber, please lance my boil,' she said.

But the barber sneered. 'Hah, I am the king's barber. I am not going to lance *your* boil!'

Tuntuni was hurt and angry. 'Just you wait! We shall see if you lance my boil or not,' said she, and went off to complain to the king.

'O king!' she said when she found him, still in bed in the royal bedroom, 'the barber isn't lancing my boil. You must punish him at once.'

The king thought this tiny bird's demand was very funny. He rolled around on his bed, roaring with laughter. And he didn't say a word to the barber.

That made Tuntuni very angry. She went to the rat and said, 'Dear Rat, dear Rat, are you home?'

The rat said:

Who's there? Tuni dear?
Come in, dear, sit, dear.
Pull up a cot,

I'll stir up a pot,
Will you dine with me, dear?

Said Tuntuni, 'I will, if you do something for me.'

Asked the rat, 'What?'

Said Tuntuni, 'When the king sleeps, gnaw a hole into his big fat tummy.'

But the rat bit his tongue and rolled his eyes and said, 'Oh no, I can't do that!'

This made Tuntuni even more angry. She went to the pussycat and said, 'Dear Pussycat, dear Pussycat, are you home?'

The pussycat said:

Who's there? Tuni dear?
Come in, dear, sit, dear.
Pull up a cot,
I'll stir up a pot,
Will you dine with me, dear?

Said Tuntuni, 'I will, if you kill Rat.'

But the pussycat said, 'I can't kill Rat now, I'm far too sleepy.'

Tuntuni was now really furious. She went to the stick and said, 'Dear Stick, dear Stick, are you home?'

The stick said:

Who's there? Tuni dear?
Come in, dear, sit, dear.

Pull up a cot,
I'll stir up a pot,
Will you dine with me, dear?

Said Tuntuni, 'I will, if you beat up Pussycat.'

But the stick said, 'Pussycat hasn't done me any harm, so why should I beat her up? I won't do it.'

So fuming and fretting Tuntuni went to the fire and said, 'Dear Fire, dear Fire, are you home?'

The fire said:

Who's there? Tuni dear?
Come in, dear, sit, dear.
Pull up a cot,
I'll stir up a pot,
Will you dine with me, dear?

Said Tuntuni, 'I will, if you burn Stick.'

But the fire said, 'I have burnt a whole lot of things today. I can't burn anything more now.'

Tuntuni was enraged and shouted at the fire. She went to the sea and said, 'Dear Sea, dear Sea, are you home?'

The sea said:

Who's there? Tuni dear?
Come in, dear, sit, dear.
Pull up a cot,

I'll stir up a pot,
Will you dine with me, dear?

Said Tuntuni, 'I will, if you put out Fire.'

But the sea said, 'That I won't do.'

Furious beyond words, Tuntuni went to the elephant and said, 'Dear Elephant, dear Elephant, are you home?'

The elephant said:

Who's there? Tuni dear?
Come in, dear, sit, dear.
Pull up a cot,
I'll stir up a pot,
Will you dine with me, dear?

Said Tuntuni, 'I will, if you drink up Sea.'

But the elephant said, 'I can't drink all that water. And besides, Sea is far too salty. My tummy will burst!'

When Tuntuni found that no one was listening to her, she finally went to the mosquito. The mosquito saw her from far and said:

Who's there? Tuni dear?
Come in, dear, sit, dear.
Pull up a cot,
I'll stir up a pot,
Will you dine with me, dear?

Said Tuntuni, 'I will, if you bite Elephant.'

Said the mosquito, 'Is that all? I'll do it right away. Let's see how thick Elephant's skin is!'

Then he called all the mosquitoes from all the lands of the earth, and told them, 'Come brothers. Let us see how thick Elephant's skin is!'

And all the mosquitoes of the world, fathers and sons and brothers and friends, set off to bite the elephant.

The sky darkened. The sun was covered. The flapping of the wings caused a storm. And the terrible humming had everyone running in fear!

And then:

The elephant said, 'I must drink up Sea's water!'

The sea said, 'I must put out Fire!'

The fire said, 'I must burn Stick!'

The stick said, 'I must beat up Pussycat!'

The pussycat said, 'I must kill Rat!'

The rat said, 'I must gnaw a hole into the king's big fat tummy!'

The king said, 'I must cut off that barber's head!'

And the barber came to Tuntuni trembling with fear and said, 'Save me, Madam Tuntuni! Come, I will lance your boil!'

And that's how Tuntuni scared the barber and got her boil cured.

HOW THE KING LOST HIS NOSE

Tuntuni the little tailor bird had built her nest in one corner of the king's garden.

One day, the king's men had put the king's gold coins out in the sun to dry. In the evening, when they took the coins back, they left one behind by mistake.

Tuntuni saw the shiny gold coin and put it in her nest. 'My! I am rich now!' she thought. 'What the king has, I too have it!'

She thought about this, and thought about this, and finally she sang:

What the king has, I too have it!
The wealth the king has, I too have it!

The king was sitting in his court. He heard Tuntuni singing, and asked, 'What is that bird saying?'

The king's men said, 'Your Majesty, the bird claims that she too has all the riches that you have.'

The king was tickled pink. He roared with laughter and said, 'Go and see what she has in her nest.'

They came back and told him, 'She has a gold coin there.'

'The coin must be mine!' said the king. 'Go and get it back.'

So they took the coin away from Tuntuni's nest.

Poor Tuntuni! What could she do? Sadly, she sang:

What a greedy king he is, he takes Tuni's money away!

The king has so much wealth, but he still takes Tuni's money away!

That made the king laugh some more. He said, 'What a stubborn little bird she is! Go and give her coin back to her.'

Tuntuni was delighted to have her riches back. She sang:

The king got scared! The king got scared!
He returned Tuni's coin because he got scared!

'NOW what is she saying?' asked the king.

'Your Majesty,' said his men, 'she is saying you gave her coin back because you are scared of her.'

This made the king furious! 'How dare she?' he shouted. 'Go catch her, I'll fry her and eat her!'

The soldiers caught poor Tuntuni and brought her before the king. He took her to his queens and told them, 'Fry this bird for my lunch today.'

The king went back to his court, leaving Tuntuni with the seven queens. 'What a beautiful bird! Let me hold her,' one of them said and took Tuntuni in her palm. Soon all the queens wanted to hold her and pet her in turn. And as she was being passed from queen to queen, Tuntuni saw her chance and flew away!

The queens were very scared! If the king came to know, he would never forgive them!

As they were wondering what to do, they saw a frog passing by. The queens quickly caught it and told one another, 'Shhh! No one must know about this! We will fry the frog and the king will think he has eaten Tuntuni!'

The king ate the frog and was very happy. He sat down on his throne and thought, 'Now that pest of a bird cannot trouble me any more!'

Just then, he heard Tuntuni singing:

What fun, what fun, the king ate a frog!
The king thinks it's Tuni, but he ate a frog!

The king jumped up from his throne, mad with anger! The little bird and his queens had made a fool of him! He, the king, had ended up eating a dirty frog!

'Guard!' shouted the king. 'Cut off the noses of all the queens!'

The guard went away and cut off the noses of all the seven queens.

Tuntuni saw this and sang:

Little Tuni sings her song, and seven queens lose their noses!
A little song from Tuni, and seven queens lose their noses!

The king said, 'Catch that wretched bird and get her here. I will swallow her whole. Let's see how she gets away this time.'

Tuntuni was brought to the court. The king took a swig of water, put the little bird in his mouth and swallowed her.

'Aha!' said everyone in admiration. 'That should fix her!'

But just then the king gave a loud belch. And with that belch, up came Tuntuni from the king's tummy and out through his open mouth, and she flew away to safety!

'Catch her! Catch her!' the king shouted, and two hundred men ran and caught poor Tuntuni again.

This time, a guard with a sword stood next to the king, so that if Tuntuni came out again, the guard would cut her head off. The king swallowed Tuntuni and put both hands over his mouth, so the little bird would not be able to get out.

Poor Tuntuni was now trapped inside the king's tummy! She started fluttering her wings in fear!

All the movement in his tummy made the king quite sick! After a little a while, he couldn't hold it back any more. Everything inside his tummy came out, and Tuntuni too!

'Guard! Guard! Kill her!' everyone shouted. 'She is getting away!'

The startled guard swung his sword, but instead of killing Tuntuni, his sword struck the king's nose, and cut it off! The king screamed, and everyone else also started screaming.

The king's doctor was called. He had to use all his medicines and bandages to save the king.

Seeing the nose-less king, Tuntuni sang:

Serves him right! Serves him right!
The king has lost his nose and it serves him right!

And she quickly flew far, far away, beyond the borders of the kingdom.

All the king's men ran to her nest and found it empty. Tuntuni was safe and free.

THE SPARROW AND THE CROW

The sparrow and the crow were very good friends.

One bright day, the two friends saw that the farmer had spread out paddy and chillies on a mat in his courtyard to dry in the sun.

'Friend, let's have a contest,' said the sparrow. 'Let's see if you can finish off all the chillies before I can eat up all the paddy.'

'I'll finish first,' said the crow.

'Oh no, I'll be the winner,' said the sparrow.

'Okay, what happens if you lose?' asked the crow.

'If I lose, you can eat my heart,' said the sparrow. 'And what happens if you lose?'

'You can eat my heart,' said the crow.

The two friends started off on the paddy and chillies. The sparrow pecked at the paddy and the crow ate the chillies in large mouthfuls.

In a little while, the crow had finished off all the chillies but the sparrow still had a long way to go.

'So, friend, what happens now?' asked the crow.

'Well, if you can be my friend and still eat up my heart, then go ahead,' said the sparrow. 'But please wash your beak before you do so, because you eat a lot of dirty things.'

'I'll be back in a minute,' said the crow and went off to the river to wash his beak.

But the river told him, 'Don't touch me with your dirty beak! Take some water out from me in a pot and wash it.'

'I'll get a pot,' said the crow and went to the potter. He perched outside the potter's hut and cawed:

Potter, potter, give me a pot,
To fill with water
To wash my beak
To eat the sparrow's heart.

'But I don't have any pots,' said the potter. 'Get me some clay. I'll make you a pot.'

So the crow went to a buffalo. He perched on a bush near where the buffalo was grazing, and he cawed:

Buffalo, buffalo, give me your horns
To dig some clay
To make a pot

To fill with water
To wash my beak
To eat the sparrow's heart.

At this, the buffalo was furious! He came charging at the crow, who fled for his life.

The crow went to a dog and cawed:

Dog, dog, kill the buffalo
To take his horns
To dig some clay
To make a pot
To fill with water
To wash my beak
To eat the sparrow's heart.

'First get me milk,' said the clever dog. 'I have to grow strong. Only then will I be able to kill the buffalo.'

So the crow went to a cow and cawed:

Cow, cow, give me milk
To feed the dog
To make him strong
To kill the buffalo
To take his horns
To dig some clay
To make a pot

To fill with water
To wash my beak
To eat the sparrow's heart.

'Get me some grass to eat,' said the cow. 'Only then can I give you milk.'

So the crow went to the meadow and cawed:

Meadow, meadow, give me grass
To feed the cow
To give me milk
To feed the dog
To make him strong
To kill the buffalo
To take his horns
To dig some clay
To make a pot
To fill with water
To wash my beak
To eat the sparrow's heart.

'There's grass all around,' said the meadow. 'Why don't you just take it?'

The crow thought about it for a while. Then he went to the blacksmith and cawed:

Blacksmith, blacksmith, give me a sickle

To cut the grass
To feed the cow
To give me milk
To feed the dog
To make him strong
To kill the buffalo
To take his horns
To dig some clay
To make a pot
To fill with water
To wash my beak
To eat the sparrow's heart.

'I don't have a fire,' said the blacksmith. 'Get me some fire, and I'll cast you a sickle.'

So the crow went to the farmer's house and sang:

Farmer, farmer, give me fire
To give the blacksmith
To cast a sickle
To cut the grass
To feed the cow
To give me milk
To feed the dog
To make him strong
To kill the buffalo
To take his horns

To dig some clay
To make a pot
To fill with water
To wash my beak
To eat the sparrow's heart.

The farmer brought fire in a pot and asked, 'How will you carry it?'

The stupid crow spread out his wings and said, 'Just pour it over my wings.'

The farmer poured all the fire in the pot on the crow's wings. The fire completely burnt up the crow. And he could not eat the sparrow's heart.

THE SPARROW AND THE TIGER

In one corner of the farmer's house hung a pot, and inside it lived Mr and Mrs Sparrow.

'Ah wife, I want to eat some *pithe*,' Mr Sparrow told Mrs Sparrow one day.

'I can't make *pithe* just like that,' said Mrs Sparrow. 'I need flour, I need jaggery, I need bananas, I need milk, and I need wood. Get me all these, and I'll make you *pithe*.'

'All right, I'll get you everything,' said Mr Sparrow, already feeling hungry but a bit worried about how to collect so many different things.

He flew to the forest and began breaking thin dry branches off the trees.

In the forest lived a huge tiger who considered Mr Sparrow his friend. He heard the sound of branches breaking and asked, 'Is that you, my friend?'

'Yes,' replied Mr Sparrow.

'What will you do with the branches?' asked the tiger.

'I need wood. Mrs Sparrow is going to make *pithe* for me,' said Mr Sparrow.

'I have never had *pithe*, though you have spoken so often about how wonderful it is,' said the tiger. 'Mrs Sparrow must make some for me too.'

'*Pithe* can't be made just like that,' said Mr Sparrow. 'You will have to get me a whole lot of things.'

'What things?' asked the tiger.

'I need flour, jaggery, bananas, milk and wood,' said Mr Sparrow.

'Go home, I will get you everything,' said the tiger.

Mr Sparrow went home and the tiger went off to the market. He just had to let out a small roar and all the shopkeepers left their shops and fled for their lives. The tiger went through all the shops, found flour, jaggery, bananas, milk, wood and a pot, and took them to the Sparrows' home.

Mrs Sparrow made some wonderful *pithes* and the Sparrows ate a whole lot of them. In fact, they could not stop themselves and ate up all of them except one.

Completely stuffed, they paused to look at the remains of the feast. They knew that the tiger would be very angry if he found that they had left only one *pithe* for him.

'What shall we do, wife?' asked Mr Sparrow quaveringly.

'Don't worry,' said Mrs Sparrow briskly. 'I have an idea.'

So Mrs Sparrow made some more *pithes* out of flour, sawdust and cowdung, and left them outside for the tiger. Then the Sparrows hid quietly in their pot.

In the evening, the tiger came, saw the *pithes* and sat down to eat at once. He ate one and said, 'Ah, this is wonderful!'

Then he put another one in his mouth. 'No, this is not so good!' he exclaimed. 'This seems to be made only out of flour!'

He took another *pithe*. He couldn't believe it. 'This is made of sawdust!' he cried. And he put another in his mouth, took one bite and spat it out angrily.

'This smells very strange!' he roared. 'Is there cowdung in this? That Sparrow is a rascal!'

Mr and Mrs Sparrow huddled close and shivered. If only the tiger would go away!

Inside the pot, Mr Sparrow suddenly felt very sneezy. 'Wife, I'm going to sneeze!' he whispered.

'Shh! Not now!' begged Mrs Sparrow.

Mr Sparrow kept quiet for a while, but soon he felt like sneezing again. Mrs Sparrow could not stop him.

The tiger had had another horrible *pithe* by now and was furious. 'This is made only of cowdung!' he cried. 'They haven't put anything else in it! When I get hold of that Sparrow, I'm going to eat him up!' He roared so angrily that the pot rattled.

Aaatchooo!

Mr Sparrow could not control his sneeze any longer.

Hearing the loud Aaatchooo! the tiger jumped up in shock.

And so powerful was the sneeze that the pot, with the Sparrows in it, fell right on his head.

The tiger couldn't figure out what was happening. Was it thunder? Or was it the sky falling on his head? He ran and ran and did not stop till he reached his home.

TALES OF FOXES

THE TIGER, THE FOX AND THE LION'S UNCLE

At the foot of the high mountains, in a little hole in a field next to a dark forest lived a goat and her kid.

The kid was quite small, and his mother did not let him step out of the hole. Whenever he wanted to go out, she said, 'Don't! Bears may catch you, tigers may carry you away and lions may eat you up!' that would frighten the kid and he would sit quietly inside the hole.

But as he grew up a bit, he became less and less afraid. When his mother was not around, he would peep out of the hole and gaze at what was around. Finally, one day, when his mother was away the kid stepped out.

Just outside his hole was a big ox eating grass. The kid had never seen such a large animal before! He looked closely at it, and saw that it had horns like his mother.

'It must be a goat,' he thought. 'It must be a goat that has grown very large by eating a lot of healthy things!'

He decided that he too wanted to become as big as this goat.

So he went shyly up to the ox and asked, 'What do you eat?'

'I eat grass,' replied the ox.

'My mother also eats grass,' said the kid. 'Why isn't she as big as you are?'

'I eat much better grass than your mother does,' said the ox kindly. 'And much more of it, too.'

'Where do you get such good grass?' asked the kid.

'Inside the forest,' said the ox.

'Will you please take me there?' asked the kid.

So the ox took him inside the forest. The grass there was delicious. The kid ate and ate. He ate as much as his tummy could hold. He ate so much he could hardly move.

When the sun began to set, the ox said, 'Come, let us go home now.'

But how could the kid go home? He could not even lift his leg! 'You go home,' he said. 'I'll stay here tonight.'

The ox went away. The kid saw that there was a hole nearby and crawled inside it for shelter.

Now this hole belonged to a fox. The fox had gone to his uncle the tiger's house for dinner. When he came back late at night, he found there was something inside his hole! The kid was black in colour, so in the dark the fox could not make out what sort of animal it was.

The fox was scared. 'Maybe it is some sort of monster!' he thought. In great fear, he asked, 'Who's there inside my hole?'

The kid was very clever. He thought quickly and said:

My beard is long, I'm bold as brass!
My jaws will make you scream with fright.
I'm the lion's uncle, Narahari Das!
I eat fifty tigers in one bite.

'Help!' screamed the fox and ran for his life. He ran and ran, and stopped only when he reached the tiger's house.

The tiger was surprised to see him again. 'What's the matter?' he asked. 'Why are you back so soon?'

'Oh, Uncle, we are done for!' panted the fox. 'A Narahari Das is sitting inside my hole. He says he eats fifty tigers in one mouthful!'

This made the tiger furious! 'What cheek!' he spluttered. 'Come along, we'll see how fifty tigers make a mouthful for Narahari Das!'

'I am not going there,' said the terrified fox. 'If he comes to eat us, you can always get away. But I can't run as fast as you do. That monster will catch me and eat me up!'

'Please don't worry, nephew,' the tiger said reassuringly. 'I won't leave you and run away.'

'Then tie me to your tail and take me there,' said the fox.

So the tiger tied the fox to his tail. 'Now he can't run off without me,' thought the fox.

But as they walked towards the fox's hole, the kid spotted them from far. He yelled at the fox, 'I gave you money to buy ten tigers, you fool! And you bring me just one, tied to your tail?'

This scared the tiger out of his wits! He thought the fox must have tricked him and brought him there for Narahari Das to eat!

He turned and ran for his life, the fox still tied to his tail. As the tiger ran, his nephew was thrown to the ground, dragged through thorns, bounced over rocks.

'Watch out, Uncle, watch out!' the fox kept shouting. The more he shouted, the more terrified the tiger was that Narahari Das was about to catch him, and the faster he ran! He did not stop till he had run fifty miles.

In the morning, the kid went home.

And the fox never forgave his Uncle Tiger.

UNCLE TIGER AND NEPHEW FOX

The fox was very angry with the tiger for having dragged him for fifty miles when the tiger escaped from Narahari Das.

'Just you wait, Uncle,' he thought to himself. 'I'll get even with you.'

The fox had stopped living in his old hole because he was scared of Narahari Das. He had found a new hole and made it his home. Next to the hole was a well. 'Aha,' thought the fox.

One day, the fox found a mat near the river and brought it home. He laid it carefully over the mouth of the well and went to visit the tiger. He said, 'Uncle, don't you want to see my new house?'

The tiger came over at once. The fox pointed at the mat covering the well and said, 'Please sit down, Uncle. I'll get you something to munch.'

The tiger was very happy at the thought of food. He sat down on the mat and—Splash!—fell into the well.

The fox shouted, 'Uncle, drink lots of water! Drink all of it up while I get the food!'

And he scampered away.

But the well did not have much water, so the tiger did not drown. He was very scared when he fell in, but he managed to climb out.

As soon as he was out, he roared, 'Where have you gone, you son of a fox? Just you wait!'

But the fox had run away long ago.

The tiger did not forget. For days and weeks, every time he spied the fox in the distance, he went leaping and roaring to catch him.

The fox was terrified. He had to stay hidden all the time. He could neither go home nor hunt for food.

After some time, the fox grew thin and weak. Finally, he decided that if he went on like this, he would surely die.

Why not then go to Uncle Tiger and see if he could please him in some way?

So the fox went to visit the tiger. When he was quite far from the tiger's home, he started bowing and calling, 'Uncle! Uncle!'

The tiger was surprised. And before he could decide what to do, the fox ran to him and fell at his feet and said, 'Uncle, it broke my heart that you have been looking all over for me but could not find me. I have come because I love you very much. You don't have to look for me any more, kill me right away!'

This confused the tiger even more. Instead of killing the fox, he scolded him, 'You wicked creature! Why did you make me fall in the well?'

The fox kept a straight face and said: 'Oh no! Could I ever make you fall in a well? The ground there was very soft, and you sat down so hard that the earth caved in. After all, is there anyone as strong and brave as you are?'

The stupid tiger was fooled by this. 'You are right, nephew,' he said, very pleased. 'I was mistaken.'

The fox and the tiger became friends again.

Or so the tiger thought.

After a while, the fox started getting bored. One day, he saw a twenty-foot-long alligator basking in the sun on the river bank. He quickly ran to the tiger and said, 'I have just bought a boat. Do come and see!'

When the tiger reached the bank, he thought that the crocodile was really a boat, and jumped up on its back.

The crocodile was furious! He caught the tiger in his jaws and dragged him into the river.

And the sly fox went home very happy.

HOW THE WEAVER MARRIED THE PRINCESS

Once upon a time there was a stupid weaver called Raja. One day, while working in the rice field with his sickle, he fell asleep. When he woke up, he found that his sickle was very hot.

The sickle had grown hot in the sun, but the stupid weaver thought it was ill and started crying. 'My sickle has fever!' he howled. 'It will surely die!'

A farmer was working in the next field. He heard the weaver crying and asked him what the matter was.

'My sickle has fever,' said the weaver.

The farmer started laughing. 'Just put the sickle in water,' he said, 'and the fever will go away.'

The water cooled the sickle down, and the weaver was very happy.

Then, one day, the weaver's mother came down with fever. Everyone told him, 'Call the doctor.'

But the weaver said, 'I know the cure.'

He took his mother to a nearby pond and forced her under the water. The more she struggled, the more firmly he held her down and said, 'Wait, you'll soon get cured.'

After a while, the weaver pulled her out of the water and found that she was quite dead. The weaver was very unhappy. He cried and cried for three days. He didn't eat anything, he didn't even go home. He just lay by the pond and wept.

The fox was the weaver's friend. He was sad to see his friend so unhappy. 'Don't cry,' he told the weaver. 'I'll get you married to a princess.'

The weaver wiped his tears and went home. After that, every day, he would ask the fox, 'What about your promise?'

'I made you a promise,' said the fox, 'so I will get you married to a princess. But first you must weave some fine cloth.'

The weaver spent the next two months weaving some beautiful cloth. When the fox came to visit him after that, he found that the weaver had made yards and yards of the most beautiful fabric.

The fox told the weaver to have a good bath and went off to ask the king for his daughter's hand.

To meet the king, the fox dressed himself like a proper gentleman, with a fine turban and a shawl, a pen stuck behind his ear and an umbrella tucked under his arm. When he reached the king's court, the king thought the fox must be someone very wise. 'What brings you here, O Wise Fox?' he asked.

'Your Majesty,' replied the fox. 'I have come to find out if you would want our Raja as your son-in-law.'

The stupid weaver's name was Raja, which means king. But the king thought the fox was talking of some real king. 'What sort of a man is your Raja?' he asked eagerly.

Said the fox:

Our Raja is handsome all right,
His house is filled with light.
He is as wise as he is well read,
With one blow, he can drop ten dead!
What more, you ask, does he do?
He clothes and feeds quite a few!

The weaver was really good-looking, which is why the fox had said, 'Our Raja is handsome all right.' The weaver was so poor that his house had no roof, so there was always either sunlight or moonlight coming in, which was why 'His house is filled with light.' But the king thought the fox was describing a splendid palace.

'He is as wise as he is well read' was also true, as the weaver was neither wise nor well read. But the king thought it meant that he was very wise and well read.

When the fox said, 'With his one blow, he can drop ten dead!' he was talking about rice plants, ten of which

the weaver could cut down with one swipe of his sickle, as could any farmer. But the king thought it meant he was very strong and brave.

The weaver tilled his field and wove cloth. People ate the rice that came from his field, and wore the clothes he made. That is why the fox had said, 'He clothes and feeds quite a few!' But the king did not know this. He thought this king the fox was talking about was a generous lord who fed and clothed the poor in his kingdom.

The king was very pleased. He gave the fox a thousand rupees as reward and told him, 'I will certainly marry my daughter to your Raja. Go and fetch him. The wedding will be held eight days from now.'

With the bag of money under his belt, the fox went dancing back to the weaver. He found him still weaving cloth. In fact, he had woven so much cloth that there was enough to make a shawl for everyone in the village.

The fox gave each villager a shawl and two rupees from the money the king had given him. He told everyone, 'Eight days from today, our Raja is getting married to the king's daughter. You are all invited to the wedding.'

The villagers were very happy for the weaver. Even though he was very stupid, Raja was a good, kind person and everyone in the village was fond of him.

Next, the fox went to all the other foxes of the village and said, 'Brothers, my friend is getting married. You are all invited. You all have to sing at the wedding.'

'Yes, yes,' howled all the foxes. 'We'll all come!'

Then the fox went to all the frogs in the village. He said, 'Brothers, my friend is getting married. You are all invited. You all have to sing at the wedding.'

'Yes, yes,' croaked all the frogs. 'We'll all come!'

After this, the fox went to all the sparrows, all the cuckoos, all the crows, all the pigeons, all the peacocks, all the mynahs, all the thrushes, all the doves, all the ducks and all the other birds. To each group he said, 'Brothers, my friend is getting married. You are all invited. You all have to sing at the wedding.'

'Yes, yes,' they all chirped and cooed and billed and twittered. 'We'll all come!'

All this work took seven days. The next night was the wedding.

The fox rented some beautiful clothes for the weaver. When Raja put them on, he looked like a real king. Everyone who had been invited gathered outside Raja's house.

When it was time, the fox set off for the king's palace with Raja, followed by the villagers, the foxes, the frogs and every kind of bird. It was a grand procession.

When they could see the palace in the distance, the fox announced loudly, 'There you see the palace lights in the distance. Wait here while I run ahead and inform the king.'

Everyone murmured in agreement.

'But first,' said the fox, 'we should let them know the groom is coming. A princess's groom should come accompanied by grand music. Let's see how loud your voices are. All of you should start singing NOW.'

Then—

Five thousand foxes howled.

Twelve thousand frogs croaked.

Seven thousand sparrows twittered.

Two thousand mynahs sang.

Three thousand crows cawed.

Eleven thousand pigeons cooed.

And all the thousands of other birds sang their own songs.

The din was TERRIBLE!

At the palace, all the king's men were scared out of their wits! They trembled and clung to one another.

When the fox reached the palace, the king asked him anxiously, 'What is all that noise?'

'Oh, our men are singing and making merry,' said the fox.

The king was very upset! He thought tens of thousands of guests had arrived. Where would he seat so many people? How would he feed so many of them? 'Oh, what should I do?' he asked the fox, after explaining his problem.

'Don't worry, O king. We do not want to inconvenience you! I will go and tell our men to go back,' said the fox. 'I will just get my Raja.'

The king was so pleased that he gave the fox five thousand rupees as reward.

The fox scampered off. With the money, he bought lots of fish and worms and sweets and other food. He took this to where everyone was waiting.

'The king loved your music and sent gifts for all of you,' he said. To the villagers, he gave as many sweets as they could eat. To the birds and frogs and foxes he gave the fish and worms and other food.

All the foxes and frogs and birds and villagers were very happy. They ate their fill and went home.

Then the fox took the weaver to the king. On the way, he told him, 'Careful! Don't open your mouth at all, or you won't get the princess!'

The king's family, courtiers and friends were very pleased with the bridegroom for he looked as handsome as promised, made no demands and did whatever he was asked to do during the wedding ceremony without a word of protest. But one thing puzzled them. They kept asking the fox, 'Why doesn't he speak?'

'His mother has just died,' explained the fox. 'He's very sad, that's why he's not speaking.'

'Oh, poor fellow!' said everyone.

At dinner, the weaver was served rice in a golden dish. Surrounding the dish were one hundred golden bowls, filled with different curries and sweets. The weaver took each bowl in his hand and sniffed at it. He could not recognize anything and had no idea which one he was supposed to eat first. So he mixed the curries and the sweets all together with the rice. He ate some of it and the rest he tied in his shawl to take back home.

Everyone asked the fox, 'Why is your Raja like this? Why did he eat everything together? Why is he wrapping up food in his shawl?'

'Our Raja always has his food at one go,' whispered the fox to them. 'And whatever he can't eat, he ties in his shawl and gives away to the poor, even the shawl. Please call someone poor.' He took the shawl from the weaver and gave it away to a poor man.

It was late by the time dinner was over, and Raja was escorted to the bedroom.

When he saw the bed, the weaver was totally baffled. It was a four-poster bed made of ivory, with a mosquito net over it. The weaver had never seen either a four-poster bed or a mosquito net. He thought that it was a house within the room, and decided to look for a way to get in and find a place to sleep.

He crawled under the bed, but there was no entrance there. Then he went all around the mosquito net looking for a door. When he couldn't find any, he decided that the entrance must be at the top. So he started climbing up one of the bedposts.

But the bedpost could not take his weight. It came crashing down, mosquito net, weaver and all.

The weaver began to cry in pain and anger. 'Oh, I worked in my field and wove cloth,' he wept. 'I was happy. Why did I have to marry the princess?'

Luckily, there was no one around except the princess and the fox. The princess cried a lot, and scolded the fox. But she was a very wise girl, and did not talk about this to anyone else. Instead, she started planning what to do.

The next morning, the princess went to the king and said, 'Father, my husband wants to show me many lovely countries all over the world. Can we go?'

The king agreed happily. He gave them lots of money and sent some of his own men to take care of them.

The princess took the weaver to another country and got many wise men to teach him lots of things. In two years, Raja the weaver became a learned and brave man.

It was then that news came that the king had died, and since he had no sons, he had named his son-in-law his successor. And the weaver, who was now no longer stupid, and the beautiful princess ruled wisely and lived happily ever after.

THE WITNESS FOX

A merchant was travelling to a distant city on his horse. On the way, he felt very sleepy. So he tied his horse to a big tree and fell asleep under the shade of its broad branches.

While he slept, a thief untied his horse and tried to slip away quietly with it.

The sound of his horse's hooves woke the merchant up. 'Where are you going with my horse?' he asked the thief.

The thief looked very puzzled and angry. He said, 'What horse are you talking about?'

The merchant was amazed. 'What do you mean?' he exclaimed. 'You are taking my horse away *and* you want to know which is my horse?'

The cunning thief made a glum face. He said, 'Be careful of what you say! You can't call this your horse when you know it is mine!'

The merchant was furious. 'I brought it from home!' he said. 'How dare you say that it belongs to you!'

'Is that so?' said the thief. 'This horse is my tree's baby. It was born just now. Don't go about making false accusations, or you're going to be in trouble.'

Seeing no way out, the merchant made the thief come with him to the king's palace. Every day, at a certain time, the king would listen to his people's complaints.

When the merchant's turn came, he said, 'Your Highness, I was sleeping with my horse tied to a tree, and this thief tried to run away with it.'

'Why were you taking his horse away?' the king asked the thief.

The thief saluted the king and said, 'Pray listen to me, Your Highness. This was never his horse. My tree just gave birth to this horse and I was taking it for a ride. This fellow was asleep under my tree. He woke up and started claiming the horse was his. He is lying, Your Highness.'

'This is very bad!' the king said to the merchant. 'This horse is his tree's baby. How can you say that it belongs to you? I see that you are a dishonest man. Go away and don't trouble me again!' He told the thief to take the horse.

As the merchant walked back to his house, he wept in sorrow. On his way, he met a fox.

Seeing the merchant crying, the fox asked him, 'What makes you so unhappy?'

'Oh, what is the point now of telling my story?' wept the merchant. 'A thief came and stole my horse. I went and complained to the king. But the thief told the king that the horse was his tree's baby! And the king believed him and gave him my horse.'

The fox made noises of sympathy. Then he said, 'There is something you can do.'

'What is it?' asked the merchant eagerly.

'Go to the king again and tell him that you have a witness, and that you can bring him to the king's court if there are no dogs around.'

So the merchant went to the king again. He said, 'Your highness, I have a witness who can prove that the horse is mine. But he can't come here because he's scared of all the dogs in your palace. If you will please lock the dogs away, I can bring my witness here.'

The king ordered his men to lock up his dogs. Then he told the merchant, 'All right, let your witness appear now.'

As soon as he got the signal from the merchant, the fox came tottering into the king's court with his eyes closed. The moment he entered the court, he leaned against a wall and started dozing off.

The king started laughing at this sight. 'Oh, it's you, Wise Fox!' he exclaimed. 'Why are you sleeping?'

The fox half-opened his eyes with great difficulty. 'Your Highness, I was up eating fish all night. That's why I'm sleepy.'

'Where did you get so many fish?' asked the king.

'The river caught fire last night,' said the fox, 'and all the fish climbed on to the bank. My friends and I spent the entire night eating fish. But there were so many of them that we still couldn't finish them off!'

On hearing this, the king laughed so hard that he nearly burst his tummy! Finally, he somehow managed to calm down enough to talk. 'I haven't heard a stranger tale in my life!' he said. 'A river on fire! These are madmen's tales!'

The fox said, 'Have you ever heard of a tree giving birth to a horse? If that is not a madman's tale, what's wrong with my story about the river being on fire?'

When he heard this, the king fell into deep thought. 'You are right,' he said at last. 'How can a tree give birth to a horse? That man must have been a cheat!'

He ordered his men to catch the thief and bring him to court in chains.

Ten soldiers went at once and caught the thief. When he was brought before the king, the king said, 'Let him get fifty whacks with a shoe!'

As soon as the king said this, all the king's men took off their shoes and started whacking the rascal on his back. After twenty-five blows, the thief started screaming. 'Let me go!' he cried. 'I'll bring the horse. I'll never do it again!'

But no one paid him any attention. After the full punishment was meted out, the king said, 'Quickly get the horse, or another fifty whacks for you.'

The thief ran off at once and returned with the horse. He was then chased out of the country in disgrace.

The merchant was overjoyed to get his horse back, and kept thanking and blessing the fox.

THE STUPID CROCODILE AND THE LEARNED FOX

A crocodile and a fox decided that they would grow vegetables together. After a lot of thought, they decided that potatoes would be the best thing to grow.

Of course you know and I know that potatoes grow underground. And the part of the plant that grows above ground cannot be eaten. But the foolish crocodile did not know this. He thought that the potato was a fruit!

In addition to being stupid, the crocodile was also greedy. So, to cheat the fox, he said, 'Whatever is above the ground is mine and everything below belongs to you.'

The fox smiled and said, 'All right.'

Months went by. The potato plants grew merrily. Finally, the time came for harvesting them.

'I'll take my share first,' said the crocodile to the fox. 'Then you can come and dig out your share.'

The crocodile cut off the plants from above the soil and hurried home with them. But when he reached home and looked closely at his share, he realized that there were only useless leaves and no potatoes!

He hurried back to the fields and saw that the fox had dug up the earth and taken all the potatoes away. 'I got deceived,' thought the crocodile. 'I'll be more careful next time.'

The next time they planned to grow paddy. The crocodile, wiser this time, said to the fox in advance, 'I'll take whatever is below the ground. You can take everything above.'

Again the fox smiled and said, 'All right.'

When the paddy was ready for harvesting, the fox came and cut the plants.

Then it was the crocodile's turn. He was very pleased. He was sure that he would find all the grains under the ground.

But what bad luck! He dug up the earth to find nothing there but useless roots!

The crocodile was livid with anger. 'Just wait and see what I do to you, you sly fox!' he said to himself. 'I won't let you touch the upper half of the plants the next time.'

The next time they grew sugarcane. This time, the crocodile said that they would both share what grew above ground, but he would get the top half and the fox would get the bottom half.

The fox smiled and said, 'All right.'

When it was time to harvest, the crocodile took the upper part of the plants and went home happily. But when he bit into his share, he discovered it was salty.

Meanwhile, the fox got the sweet and juicy part of the sugarcane.

The crocodile was so angry that he told the fox that he would not grow vegetables with him again.

■

The crocodile thought and thought about why the fox was outwitting him every time. Finally, he realized why they were different. 'The fox is very learned and I can't read. That is why he is able to cheat me so easily,' he thought to himself.

After pondering over the matter for some more time, the crocodile decided that he would send his seven sons to the fox and ask him to educate them.

He arrived at the fox's house with his seven sons the very next morning. The fox was in his hole eating crabs.

'O wise and learned fox! Are you home?' cried the crocodile.

The fox came out of his hole and asked, 'What brings you here, my friend?'

'I've brought my seven sons,' said the crocodile. 'They can't even read. How will they survive in this world? Please teach them how to read and write.'

'I would love to teach them,' said the fox. 'It will take me seven days to educate your seven sons.'

The crocodile was very pleased. He left his sons with the fox and went back home.

The fox made all the seven sons sit down in a row, and thought a while. Then he smiled. He took one of the sons aside and told him to repeat what was written on the board.

Seat, beat, heat, wheat,
Baby crocs I love to eat!

As the crocodile started to read, the fox pounced on him and ate him up!

The next day, the crocodile came to see how his sons were progressing. 'Hello, fox,' he cried. 'I have come to see how my sons are!'

For a moment, the fox panicked. What was he to do? He was one son short. But then he had an idea.

He peeped out of his hole and greeted the crocodile. 'Your sons are studying in separate rooms,' he said. 'I will not disturb them all, but I will show them to you one at a time.'

The crocodile agreed.

The fox took the baby crocodiles out of the hole one at a time and showed them to their father. He showed the sixth one twice, and the crocodile was satisfied that all seven sons were well and studying hard.

The crocodile went home, thinking that his seven sons would soon become great scholars.

As soon as the crocodile had left, the fox took one more of the babies aside and told him to repeat what was written on the board:

Seat, beat, heat, wheat,
Baby crocs I love to eat!

And the fox swallowed the second baby crocodile too.

When the crocodile came to visit him the next day, the fox showed him all his sons and he showed the fifth one three times. And the crocodile went home pleased.

In this way, the fox ate up the baby crocodiles and deceived their father for six days, until there was only one son left. That day, he showed this last son to the crocodile seven times.

The crocodile went away, happy that the seven days of education would be over soon and he could take his learned sons home, and the fox ate up the last son as well.

The next morning, Mrs Fox was very worried. 'What should we do now?' she said. 'When the crocodile comes, we will have no more sons to show him. If he doesn't see his babies, he will surely eat us up.'

'He can eat us only if he is able to catch us,' said the fox. 'There is a deep forest on the other side of the river. Let's go there. The crocodile will never be able to find us.'

So the fox and his wife left their old home and went away.

A little while later, the crocodile reached the fox's old home. He called out, 'O wise fox!' several times, but there was no response. He went into the hole to look for the fox, but found that the fox and his wife had left. There was nothing there but the bones of the baby crocodiles.

Furious, the crocodile ran around looking for the fox. He reached the bank of the river and saw the fox and his wife swimming across.

'Just wait, you rascals!' said the crocodile and dived into the river.

Crocodiles can swim much faster than foxes. Very soon, he caught up with the foxes, who had just reached the other side. Mrs Fox had already climbed on to land.

The crocodile grabbed hold of the fox's hind foot with his sharp teeth, just as the fox placed his front feet on land.

When the fox felt the crocodile biting his foot, he called out to his wife, 'Someone is pulling at my stick. Chase him away!'

The foolish crocodile thought that he was biting the fox's stick instead of his foot and he let it go.

As soon as his foot was free, the fox jumped on to the bank and ran for his life. Soon he was inside the deep woods where nobody would be able to find him.

■

The crocodile spent many days hunting for the fox, but in vain. Then he sat at home and thought for a long time until a plan slowly formed in his mind.

The next day, he lay flat on the river bank pretending to be dead.

Soon after, the fox and his wife came there to catch crabs and saw the crocodile lying still. 'He's dead! Let's eat him!' cried Mrs Fox in glee.

'Wait!' said the fox. 'Let us first make sure he is dead.'

The fox went a little closer to the crocodile and examined him closely. He said to his wife, 'No. He is too dead for us to eat. We eat crocodiles which are only slightly dead and which move a little!'

'Let me move a little,' thought the crocodile. 'Otherwise they won't come to eat me.' And he twitched his tail a bit.

Seeing his tail move, the foxes had a good laugh. 'There! He is moving! He is not dead!' the fox said. And the two of them fled into the woods.

'I was cheated again,' thought the crocodile. 'Next time I'll surely catch them.'

■

The crocodile knew where the fox and his wife went to drink water. He thought that he would hide there and wait for them. So he swam to that part of the river, and hid in the water under some overhanging leaves.

When the foxes came to the river, the fox noticed that there were no fish in the water. Usually the river had plenty of fish. He realized that the crocodile was hiding somewhere there.

He said to his wife, 'No, the water is too clean here. Let's go to a place where the water is muddy.'

The silly crocodile started moving furiously to disturb the soil and make the water muddy.

Seeing this, the foxes ran away laughing.

'Foiled again!' thought the crocodile angrily.

He continued to lurk around by the river for several days, hoping that the foxes would show up.

Some days later, the foxes came to the river. The crocodile, as he lay hidden in the reeds, could hear them talking to each other.

'I haven't had crabs for so many days,' said Mrs Fox hungrily.

But the fox was still wary because he knew the crocodile could be there. So he stood by the water and said to Mrs Fox in a clear, loud voice, 'I don't think there are any crabs here. Otherwise I would have seen some floating.'

The crocodile didn't want the foxes to go away. So he quickly put the tip of his tail out of the water and floated it a bit, hoping that the foxes would think it was a crab.

But the fox wasn't fooled this time either. He and his wife left without getting into the water.

By this time the crocodile was thoroughly ashamed of himself. He moved to a different part of the river and never showed up again.

TALES OF A CAT

MAJANTALI SARKAR

Once upon a time, in a village, there lived two cats. One of them lived in a milkman's house. There he fed on milk, curd, cheese, butter and cream.

The other cat lived with a fisherman, who gave him nothing to eat. He only got kicked and beaten from time to time.

The milkman's cat was very fat. He walked with his chest out and his head held high.

The fisherman's cat was very skinny. When he tried to walk, he would stumble and fall. All he wanted was to be as fat as the milkman's cat.

One day the thin cat said to the fat cat, 'Brother, you are invited to our house for dinner.'

This was just a trick. The fisherman's cat never got anything to eat. How could he invite someone else to dinner? But he had a cunning plan. 'When the milkman's cat comes to my house, he will get so badly beaten that he will surely die,' thought the skinny cat. 'And then I can go and stay in his place!'

The plan worked. As soon as the milkman's cat entered the fisherman's house, all the people there shouted, 'Oh no! It's that milkman's cat! It steals all his milk and cream! It has come here to steal our fish! Beat the rascal up!'

They beat him up so badly that the poor cat died.

The skinny cat was so sure that the plan would work that he had already reached the milkman's house. He started living there and had plenty of milk and cream. He got fat in very little time. He also stopped talking to the other cats from surrounding villages. And he gave himself a grand new name. If anyone asked him what he was called, he would say, 'I am Majantali Sarkar.'

■

One day Majantali Sarkar took a pen and a piece of paper and went for a stroll. After walking for some time, he reached the woods, where he saw three tiger cubs playing. He chased them and shouted, 'Pay up your taxes!'

When the tiger cubs saw his pen and paper and heard him shout, they got very scared. They quickly ran to their mother.

'Mother! Come here!' they said when they reached their home. 'Come and see who has come and what he wants to say.'

The tigress came and asked the cat, 'Who are you? Where have you come from and what do you want?'

'I am the king's minister, Majantali Sarkar,' said the cat. 'You live on the king's land. You have to pay tax.'

'I don't even know the meaning of the word "tax",' said the tigress. 'We only live in the forest and eat up whoever comes here. Why don't you wait a little, till the tiger comes back?'

Majantali Sarkar sat under a tall tree and looked around. A little while later, he saw the tiger coming towards the lair. He left his pen and paper on the ground and quickly climbed up to the top of the tree.

The tigress told the tiger what Majantali Sarkar had told her. You can't imagine how angry the tiger was! He let out a fearsome roar. 'Where is the scoundrel?' he bellowed. 'I'll break his neck!'

'What is it, tiger?' asked the cat from the top of the tree. 'Won't you pay your tax?'

The tiger gnashed his teeth and snarled at the cat. Then he leapt up to the top of the tree, but he couldn't catch Majantali.

The cat was not only nimble, but very smart. He had selected a thin branch to sit on, which could not bear the tiger's weight. So the tiger couldn't get on to it.

The tiger was furious! He gave a big jump, but slipped and fell. His head got stuck between two branches, his neck broke and he came crashing to the ground and died.

Majantali quickly climbed down and scratched the tiger's face with his claws.

Then he called the tigress. 'See what I have done,' he said. 'I can't tolerate disobedience!'

When she saw what had happened, the tigress was terrified. 'Please don't kill me,' she begged the cat. 'I'll be your slave.'

'All right, I won't harm you,' said Majantali. 'Just do your work properly and give me plenty to eat.'

The cat started staying in the tiger's home. He ate a lot and rode on the backs of the cubs when he wanted to go anywhere. The cubs were scared of Majantali. They thought that he was someone very important.

■

One day, the tigress said to him, 'My lord! There are only small animals in this forest. They are not enough to satisfy your hunger. On the other side of the river is a dense forest that has larger animals. Let us all go and stay there.'

'That's a good idea,' said the cat. 'Let's all go across the river to the other part of the forest.'

The tigress and her cubs swam across the river and soon reached the other side. But where was Majantali? The tigress and her cubs looked back and saw Majantali Sarkar in the middle of the river, struggling to stay afloat. Cats can't swim! The river was carrying him far downstream and the waves kept lashing at him.

Majantali knew that if two more waves hit him he would surely die. Fortunately, one of the cubs came to his rescue. He swam across the river and saved the cat. But Majantali pretended to be angry with the cub.

'Fat-head! Idiot!' he shouted as soon as they reached the other bank. 'Just see what you have done! I was doing some complicated calculations in my mind. You dragged me here before I could complete them. I was counting all the waves, all the fish and all the droplets of water in the river. You nitwit! You spoilt all my calculations! If I can't present them to the king, just wait and see what I do to you!'

When the tigress heard him, she quickly ran up. 'Majantali, please forgive my son for his mistake. He is uneducated and stupid. He didn't know what he was doing,' she said.

'This time I forgive him,' said the wily cat. 'But this is his last chance.' Then he started looking for a place in the sun where he could dry himself.

The forest was so dense that it did not let in any sunlight. Majantali had to climb up a tree to sun himself. From the top of the tree he saw a dead buffalo in the distance. He went and scratched the buffalo's face, called the tigress and said to her, 'Come here quickly! I've killed a buffalo for all of us.'

The tigress and her cubs ran up and saw the dead buffalo lying there. The four of them dragged it to a safe spot with great difficulty. 'My goodness! Majantali must be terribly strong to have killed such a big buffalo,' thought the tigress.

■

One day, the tigress said to Majantali, 'There are big elephants and rhinoceroses in the jungle. Let's go and kill some of them.'

'Let's go today,' agreed the cat.

He set off with the tigress and her cubs to kill elephants and rhinoceroses. On the way, the tigress asked Majantali, 'How will you kill the animals? Will you hide, watch and then spring on your prey or will you run around in the forest, scare the beasts and then kill them?'

'No beast will get scared if I run around,' thought Majantali. So he said, 'I'll stay in hiding while you all chase the animals.'

'That's a good idea,' said the tigress, 'since we won't be able to kill them ourselves. Come on, my cubs! Let's chase the beasts across the forest!'

Then the tigress and her cubs went to the other side of the forest. There they roared fiercely and frightened all the animals. When Majantali heard the animals bellow, he went and sat under a tree, trembling in fear.

A little while later, Majantali heard a hedgehog approaching. He hid under the root of a tree. In his nervous state even the hedgehog seemed very threatening. He was so intent on hiding from the hedgehog that he did not notice the ground trembling.

Just then an elephant came by and trampled over the roots. Poor Majantali! His tummy burst open and he lay there dying.

After running around for a long time, the tigress thought, 'Majantali must have killed several animals by now. Let me go and see him.' When she saw the state that he was in, she was very surprised. 'What on earth has happened to you?' she asked.

'You sent me such small animals to kill. I laughed so much that my tummy burst!' said Majantali.

And that was the last thing he ever said.

TRANSLATOR'S NOTE

These are stories I read out to my daughter when she was small. My parents read out the same stories to me when I was little and I am sure my grandparents did the same for my parents. A man of science, a writer, violinist and composer, printing technologist and painter, Upendrakishore Roychoudhury is remembered most today for his writings. He lived in the late nineteenth century and early twentieth century and his greatest contribution was in the field of children's literature in Bengal. His stories have entertained several generations of Bengali children. He is best remembered for the fantasy *Goopy Gyne Bagha Byne*, the simple tales of *Tuntunir Boi* and children's versions of the epics Ramayana and Mahabharata. He also illustrated most of his books.

Goopy Gyne Bagha Byne was made into a delightful film by Upendrakishore Roychoudhury's grandson Satyajit Ray, who is perhaps the greatest film director that India has produced. *Goopy Gyne Bagha Byne* was one of the most popular Bengali films ever made. As children we loved the film. The characters were adorable, the music was out of this world and the dance that the ghosts danced was a delightful play of light and shadow and was something we had never seen before.

As a translator, I did not face too many problems. Fortunately, the original text was written in a simple form of Bengali (which is of course one of the reasons Upendrakishore's books still delight Bengali children more than a century after they were written). Some classic Bengali texts—even those written for children—are difficult to translate because of their complexity. They are filled with words, idioms and metaphors that are no longer in common use today, posing a bigger challenge to the translator.

I had to set my own beliefs and experiences aside and directly convey to the reader what the author had to say. Then there were some words that could not be translated. '*Pithe*' is a Bengali sweet made of flour, sugar and milk. There is no equivalent word in the English language. I left it as '*pithe*'.

I had to be true to both the languages because there are cultural differences between the two. *Ghangasur* in Bengali sounds all right. The name implies a certain kind of monster. But in English the word has no appeal. I changed it to 'Ghangosaur'.

I ran into difficulty with the poems. I had to stick to their literal meaning or deviate slightly and make them rhyme. I couldn't do both. I decided to make them rhyme.

Translating the book was a labour of love. I hope you enjoy the story of Goopy and Bagha as much as I did. I hope the spirited tailor bird Tuntuni , the stupid tiger, the wily fox and the foolish weaver make their way into your hearts. I do wish more and more children get to enjoy the wit, magic and mystery woven into these unforgettable tales.

***Swagata Deb** is a PhD in Physics from IIT Delhi. She has been a scientist and teacher, and is today a children's author, painter and Reiki teacher. She lives in Gurgaon with her husband, daughter and a playful cocker spaniel.*

PUFFIN CLASSICS

Goopy Gyne Bagha Byne and Other Stories

With Puffin Classics, the story isn't over
when you reach the final page.
Want to discover more about the author
and his world?
Read on . . .

CONTENTS

AUTHOR FILE

NAME: Upendrakishore Roychoudhury (early name was Kamadaranjan Roy)

BORN: 10 May, 1863 in a little village called Moshua in Kishorgonj district in Eastern Bengal (now a part of Bangladesh)

FATHER: Kalinath Roy, later adopted by a relative Hari Kishore Roy Chowdhury, who was a zamindar in the Mymensingh district

DIED: 20 December 1915 at fifty-two years of age in Giridih in Bihar (now Jharkhand)

EDUCATION: He passed the Entrance Examination in 1880 with a scholarship from Mymensingh Zila School. He studied for some time at Presidency College, which was affiliated to Calcutta University at that time. However, he graduated with a BA degree from Vidyasagar College, which was known as Calcutta Metropolitan University.

PERSONAL LIFE: Father of the celebrated nonsense writer Sukumar Ray and grandfather of the internationally famous film-maker and author Satyajit Ray, Upendrakishore Roychoudhury was extraordinarily gifted. He was a prolific writer, a brilliant artist, a musician par excellence, a man of science, and at the same time a deeply religious man. The luxuriant green fields and forests, the streams and ponds of his childhood home, left a deep impact on him—an impact that stayed with him forever. He moved to Calcutta and spent his adult life there, but his childhood days are reflected in his writings. He was an active member of the Brahmo Movement, which led the cultural advancement of Bengal. His friend Rabindranath Tagore and he represented the peak of the Bengal Renaissance. As a writer he is best known for his contribution to Bengali children's literature.

MAN OF SCIENCE: In the field of publishing, he is still remembered in India and abroad for the introduction of half-tone block making—which began a new era of printing high-fidelity black-and-white and colour photographs. He experimented with the process of block making and many of his articles on block making were published in Britain. He started one of the most popular publishing houses in Kolkata named U.Ray & Sons.

LITERARY GENIUS: Upendrakishore's greatest contribution has been in children's literature. Some of his most prominent and admired works include the fantasy *Goopy Gyne Bagha Byne* and simple tales for children in *Tuntunir Boi* (The Book of Tuntuni). He also rewrote the Ramayana and the Mahabharata to make them comprehensible for children. The language he used for his stories was simple. It could be used by adults to read out bedtime stories to children. He himself illustrated most of his books. He also wrote enchanting science articles for children. He launched the extremely popular children's magazine *Sandesh* in 1913, which was resurrected in 1961 by his grandson Satyajit Ray and is still published today. The magazine was named after the popular Bengali sweet which in Sanskrit means 'news', showing Upendrakishore's love of wordplay.

GOOPY GYNE BAGHA BYNE, THE MOVIE SERIES

Upendrakishore Roychoudhury's fantasy tale of Goopy and Bagha—two highly 'gifted' artists—was made into a highly successful film by Upendrakishore's grandson Satyajit Ray in 1969. Ray made a sequel in 1980 from a story he wrote himself—Hirak Rajar Deshe (In the Land of the Diamond King). In 1992, a third film *Goopy Bagha Phire Elo* (Goopy and Bagha Back Again) was directed by Satyajit's son Sandip Ray, from a story by Satyajit.

The films of the series have won many national as well as international awards, such as: Award for Best Direction, New Delhi, 1968; President's Gold and Silver Medals, New Delhi, 1970; Silver Cross, Adelaide, 1969. Best Director, Auckland, 1969; Merit Award, Tokyo, 1970; Best Film, Melbourne, 1970.

Goopy Gyne Bagha Byne has won many national and international awards, including the Indian President's Gold Medal for Best Director.

The animated film *Goopi Gawaiya Bagha Bajaiya* (2013) was directed by Shilpa Ranade, and also won several national and international awards.

Sandip Ray wants to make another film in the series. He has received many requests to make a fourth *Goopy-Bagha* movie.

TUNTUNIR BOI (THE BOOK OF TUNTUNI)

There are many Bengali folk tales about Tuntuni. These are delightful little stories about a clever bird that outsmarts everyone who tries to upset her.

Is Tuntuni a real bird?

Yes, it is. It is the local name for the common tailor bird. The scientific name for this species is *Orthotomus sutorius*. It is a songbird found across tropical Asia, popular for its nest made of leaves sewn together. Although they are shy birds and hidden behind vegetation, their loud calls are familiar and give away their presence. The tailor bird has a long, upright tail, a greenish upper-body plumage and rust-coloured forehead and crown. Tuntunis are typically found in open farmland, scrub, forest edges and gardens. Their song is a loud '*cheeup-cheeup-cheeup!*' repeated several times and with variations depending upon the locality.

Tuntunir Boi, published in 1910, is still treasured and read out to children in most Bengali homes. You will find many of the stories in this book.

Tuntuni's stories are unlike the traditional legends, which often have a moral lesson to deliver. Most of the stories show how Tuntuni outwits its rivals and enemies. The stories are great fun and are quite unforgettable.

The Wily Fox

You will find that many of the characters in the book are animals. All children love animals and when we give them names and assign various qualities to them, it boosts their imagination. The fox has a special place in children's literature. When you think of a fox, what words come to your mind? Cunning, clever, sly, wily, wicked?

The fox appears in many cultures, usually in folklore. However, there are slight variations in the way in which they are depicted. In western folklore and in Persian tales, foxes are a symbol of cunning and treachery. In Asian folklore, foxes sometimes have magical powers with which they can either create wonder or bring ruin.

Nine-tailed foxes appear in Chinese folklore and mythology. They could be a good or a bad omen. In Finland, the *aurora borealis* or Northern Lights are known as Revontulet (fox fires), because it was believed that the lights were produced by a fox, painting the sky with its tail as it ran across.

The fox appears in *Aesop's Fables* and in *The Canterbury Tales.* The fox also appears as a character in *The Gingerbread Man, Chicken Licken, The Sly Red Fox and the Little Red Hen* and *Fantastic Mr Fox.*

Did you know?

Foxes belong to the dog family Canidae, hence they are known as canids.

Several cars have been named after foxes, such as the Volkswagen's Urban Fox and the Audi's Fox.

Foxes don't kill for fun. They kill in order to survive. Some nights are better for hunting. So, given the opportunity, they kill surplus food and bury it for future use.

STORIES ABOUT HUNCHBACKS

Where did the idea of Granny Hunchback come from? Artists and writers often use physical deformities to make a point. And a hunched back has captivated their imagination more than any other deformity. However, while most hunchbacked characters in art and literature are portrayed as evil, Upendrakishore's Granny Hunchback was a brave and clever woman!

The following are some familiar characters that have immortalized the 'hunchback' in literature and film.

- Manthara in the Ramayana was the maid who convinced Queen Kaikeyi that the throne of the kingdom of Ayodhya belonged to her son Bharat, and that her step-son, crown-prince Rama should be exiled.
- Quasimodo in *The Hunchback of Notre-Dame* (1831) was born with a hunchback and was feared by the townspeople as a sort of monster but he actually is a pure soul.
- Although in the original novel *Franstentein,* Dr Frankenstein does not have a hunchbacked assistant, several films based on the novel feature Igor—*Young Frankenstein* (1974), *The Nightmare Before Christmas* (1993), *Frankenweenie* (2012) and so on. In a new film adaptation of the novel, *Victor Frankenstein*, the story is told from Igor's perspective. Daniel Radcliffe—who played Harry Potter—plays Igor.
- Tom from the *Harry Potter* book and film series was a landlord and innkeeper, and the barman of the Leaky Cauldron.

SOME THINGS TO THINK ABOUT

- In the story *Goopy Gyne Bagha Byne*, Goopy's father Kanu Kyne throws his own son out of the house to save his business. Do you think this act by Goopy's father is justified? Later on, even after becoming successful enough, Goopy thinks of his parents first and chooses to help them without any grudge. What does this indicate about Goopy? Does our society reflect these values anymore?
- In many of his short stories for children, Upendrakishore included animals that could talk like human beings and possessed human traits. What do you think could be the purpose of this? Can you think of other such children's fiction writers who used animals to ridicule the follies of human beings?
- The animals in Upendrakishore's stories seem to possess intellect and reasoning like human beings, and, in some stories like 'Tuntuni and the King', they prove to be smarter. Do you feel that a world where humans, animals, birds and insects could speak to one another would have been a better world?
- In the story 'Ghangosaur's Tale', the monster is depicted as a horrible creature: one-third bird, one-third beast and one-third demon with a repulsive face and vicious temper. Can you think of other such mythical monsters that you might have read or heard about?
- In 'The Monkey Prince', we learn that we should not go by someone's looks. The seventh prince, born as a monkey, proves to be intelligent and kind-hearted, while the other princes are jealous and stupid individuals. Can you think of any other story that portrays a similar idea?
- You were introduced to Upendrakishore's magical world of talking animals, horrible monsters and clever birds. Can you create your own story on similar lines?

Read More in Puffin Classics

The Room on the Roof
Ruskin Bond
Introduction by Anita Nair

A classic story of adolescence and coming of age that has mesmerized readers for over fifty years.

Rusty, a sixteen-year-old Anglo-Indian boy, is orphaned, and has to live with his English guardian in the claustrophobic European part of town, in Dehra Dun. Unhappy with the strict ways of his guardian, Rusty runs away from home to live with his Indian friends. Plunging for the first time into the dream-bright world of the bazaar, Hindu festivals and other aspects of Indian life, Rusty is enchanted . . . and is lost forever to the prim proprieties of the European community . . .

Written when the author was himself seventeen, this moving story of love and friendship, presented in an exciting new format with an evocative introduction by bestselling author Anita Nair, will be enjoyed by a whole new generation of readers.

Read More in Puffin Classics

Wordygurdyboom!
The Nonsense World of Sukumar Ray
Translated from the Bengali by Sampurna Chattarji
Introduction by Ruskin Bond
Illustrated by Sukumar Ray

***'If you hear this you will find your heads are getting muddled,
Some of you will fathom fully, some will stay befuddled.'***

The Bengali language has never been quite so much a living, breathing creature of whimsy as in Sukumar Ray's hands, and his creations—wild and wicked, dreamy and delirious—have thrilled children and adults alike. This selection offers you the best of his world—pun-riddled, fun-fiddled poetry from *Abol Tabol* and *Khai-Khai*, stories of schoolboy pranks (*Pagla Dashu*) and madcap explorers (*Heshoram Hushiyarer Diary*), and the unforgettable harum-scarum classic of *Haw-Jaw-Baw-Raw-Law*, presented here for the first time in its entirety. All the stories and poems are accompanied by Sukumar Ray's inimitable illustrations.

Sampurna Chattarji's lively translation captures the magical nonsense groove of the Bengali original through a freewheeling play of sound and sense. With a sparkling new introduction by Ruskin Bond, this book is sure to captivate Sukumar Ray's fans and win him a whole new generation of admirers.

Read More in Puffin Classics

The Mystery of Munroe Island and Other Stories
Satyajit Ray
Translated from the Bengali by Indrani Majumdar
Introduction by Victor Banerjee

Classic sci-fi stories from a master storyteller.

Join Professor Trilokeshwar Shonku, eccentric genius and scientist, on an incredible world tour as he confronts a daring doppelganger, undertakes an experiment to create pure gold, unravels the mystery of a scientist's loss of memory and visits an unknown island to look for an amazing fruit, amongst other escapades. What is the message in the mysterious papyrus found in Cairo and why did scientists go missing in the deep jungle of Congo? Is there any truth about the sightings of the UFO and what happens when he takes an extraordinary animal to Koblenz in Germany? Featuring the indomitable Professor Shonku and a bunch of madcap characters, this brilliant new translation brings alive the magic and charm of Satyajit Ray's imaginative world. Get ready for some hair-raising fun with the weird and wonderful Professor Shonku, whose exploits have held readers spellbound for over five decades.